Thrust

VICTORIA ASHLEY

THRUST
Copyright © 2014 Victoria Ashley
All rights reserved.

Cover by
CT Cover Creations

Model: Lance Jones
Photographer: LJ Photography

Edited by
Charisse Spiers

Interior Design and Formatting by
Christine Borgford
www.perfectlypublishable.com

Chapter One

Calla

LETTING OUT A SATISFIED BREATH, my eyes explore the apartment, taking in the vast living space that is soon to be decorated with mine and Tori's things. *6th floor—room 629.*

We've been saving up to get into this building for over a year now, and being here in this beautiful room—with this gorgeous view—is the most amazing feeling of accomplishment that I've ever felt. I'm seriously so happy that I could scream my ass off . . . but it's late and I don't want to wake any of our new neighbors. I hate bad first impressions. They're so hard to fix and get past. They're ugly.

Standing here in this living room clearly confirms that mine and Tori's photography careers are going in the right direction. We're on the fast road to kicking ass. When you work your ass off and put thought and passion into the things you want, they'll eventually come to you, at least, that's what I've been telling myself since graduation. So far I haven't proven my words to be wrong.

"Holy shit!" Tori's voice echoes throughout the space as she pokes her head out of her new bedroom, catching my attention. "I still can't get over how ginormous these rooms are. These two bedrooms put together are like the whole size of our last apartment. This is insane and I love it. I'm in love, and right now I feel like we are two badass chicks. We kick ass. Damn, this feeling is so good. I need to celebrate." She reaches out her hand and waves her fingers. "Give me that bag of chips over there on the counter. There's no celebration like a celebration with Funyuns and wine. Give me. Give me. Hurry."

I look behind me, over my shoulder, and reach for the family size bag of Funyuns—Tori's addiction. I shake it in front of me, teasing her. "When the hell did you have the time to unpack these?" Raising a curious brow, I toss her the bag. "There's not one other thing in this whole apartment that is unpacked, not even the wine. You're insane. That's the only logical answer to that question, you damn Funyun junky."

"Are you kidding? I didn't *unpack* these, I rode in the U-Haul with these in my lap. I need some kind of motivation to deal with all this." She motions around at the pile of boxes. "So . . . you're welcome."

I watch in amusement as she pops a Funyun into her mouth and closes her eyes, moaning as she chews it. She leans her head back, shaking her brown hair behind her. She almost looks like she's having a mini orgasm.

"Alright," I say, with a disgusted shake of my head. "If you're done making love to that chip, it would be nice to focus on unpacking the things we might need for the night. I don't think watching you make love to your bag of chips is going to keep me entertained enough. Not after all the crap I've been through today."

She shrugs her shoulders, shaking my words off while grabbing another handful. "Give me ten. I'll be back." She disappears into her room, shutting the door behind her.

"Great, you sneaky asshole." Exhaling, I plop down onto the couch and reach for my cell phone to check the time. It's already ten past ten. I doubt Tori will be leaving that room any-time tonight. She's been doing nothing, but complaining about being tired, and this and that hurting since we started moving our things early this morning. She's got her bed and her chips. Apparently that's all she needs.

I lay here for a few minutes allowing myself to smile as I look around me. I feel like a kid that just wants to run around the whole apartment and touch *everything.* I don't, because it might look a little silly for a twenty- four year old; especially one that is so tired that I can't even manage to walk straight right now.

"I need some wine," I mumble to myself. I look over the couch at the kitchen. There's boxes piled so high that I can't even see the fridge. "That's no damn good."

It's a good thing this building has a bar and restaurant downstairs on the main floor. I love that about this place. Just imagine: work hard, come home, relax, and throw back a few drinks at the bar. Then, all you have to do is crawl your way back to your apartment and smile up at the *normal* people that are walking by and pretend that you're A-Okay.

Sitting up, I reach for my purse and pull out my wallet. "Hey, I'm going downstairs to grab a drink. You want any-thing?"

"Nope! Brad is on his way," Tori screams from her room. "We have better things planned, so you might want to stay gone for a while."

"Alright then," I say loudly. "I might or might not be back, so if I run away just remember that it's your fault completely."

Once I get down to the bar, my mouth is practically wa-tering by the time I sit down and wave the attractive bartender over.

Out of breath, the bartender smiles while leaning over the

bar. "What can I get you . . . ?"

I smile and give him what he's looking for. "Calla."

He pulls his hand through his messy, blonde hair and grabs for an empty glass. "What can I get you, Calla?"

Pulling out my wallet, I open it to my ID and set it down in front of me while thinking. "I was in the wine kind of mood, but . . . maybe I've changed my mind." I glance down at the drink menu in front of me and point at something blue. "I'm going to be adventurous tonight. Give me that." I pause to look up at his nametag. "Dane."

Dane lets out a small laugh while making a face. "Alright, Ms. Adventurous. One of those coming right up."

I'm caught up in running my fingers through my thick, blonde hair, to get some kind of fuzz out, when I hear the stool next to me scrape against the floor as it's pulled out from the bar.

Ignoring it, I continue to pick at my hair, fighting it. "What the hell are you? Get out," I grunt.

A deep chuckle causes me to pause. "Am I getting kicked out already? I haven't even done anything yet. Oh, and I'm a man by the way. I thought that part was pretty clear."

I push out a small laugh and shake my head. "Are you sure about that?" I tease. Gripping onto the bar, I start to spin my stool around to get a look at this *man*. "Anyone can have a . . ."

My words catch in my throat and I almost fall back when my eyes set on the *man* beside me. He's definitely all man; the sexiest kind that there is. *Holy shit. I must have done something good today.* Talk about being rendered speechless.

I quickly compose myself and clear my throat before continuing. "A deep voice." I swallow and look up to meet his face. "And a perfect, masculine jawline with just the right amount of stubble." My eyes trail lower to see his broad chest being hugged by a white shirt. "A firm chest and . . ." My eyes are going lower. Why are they going lower? "Um . . . a nice package." I nod my head, turning red as I realize that I just admitted that all aloud. "Definitely all man. Well this is awkward."

Giving me a sexy smirk, he nods at Dane as he sets my drink down in front of me.

"Here you are, Ms. Adventurous. Enjoy." Dane winks before looking beside me at the sexy man that is now placing a gym bag down by his feet. "A draft tonight, Kyan?"

"Absofuckinglutely." He smiles at me, keeping his eyes on mine as he continues to speak to Dane. He has such a powerful gaze that I find my eyes locked tight with his amber ones. "Make it two."

"Sure thing, man." He slaps the bar and walks away to fetch two beers.

Pulling my eyes away, I reach out faster than I've ever moved in my life and reach for the blue drink. Kyan—I guess his name is—carefully watches me as I down half of it without stopping for a breath. When you feel like a fool . . . you drink. Fast. Very fast.

"You're new here, Ms. Adventurous." He raises an eyebrow, watching me as I finally pull away from my drink that tastes just like juice. So much for being adventurous. "Is that your real name or just due to that really strong drink you've got there?"

Focusing on his gorgeous, carefree smile, I start to relax and feel more at ease. "It's due to my drink, though sadly it doesn't live up to it." I feel my eyes wandering over his body again, taking in his tattooed, muscular arm. His right arm is covered in a sleeve of tattoos, while the other one looks to be clean and firm. He must workout really hard at that gym. "My name is Calla."

He digs his teeth into his bottom lip and blindly scoots one of the beers in front of me and one in front of him as Dane drops them off. "Calla," he says smoothly. "That's a sexy name. I could definitely get used to moaning that out."

Oh my . . . what! My heart begins to beat rapidly while trying to pry my eyes away from his sexy as sin mouth. How are his lips so full and smooth? Would I get in trouble for licking them? *Yes, Calla! Really?* "Is that some kind of pick up line?" I ask, somewhat hoping that it is.

He takes a swig of his beer, looking at me over the rim. When he pulls his beer away, a sexy grin is taking over his mouth. "Nah, I've never said that before. Just stating the truth."

Now I'm the one pulling my bottom lip into my mouth. Turning away, I reach for the beer in front of me. "Is this supposed to be my adventure?"

He stands up. "Sure. If you can keep up with me."

I sit here for a second, smiling like an idiot as he walks over to one of the empty pool tables and starts setting it up.

Looks like I'll be playing pool. It's been a little while, but I have faith that I'm still pretty decent. My dad took me to bars a lot on the weekends while he watched football with his buddies. It was a fun childhood. Oh the memories!

I take out some cash and call Dane over so I can pay for my drink. Dane takes one look at me and shakes his head before nodding over in Kyan's direction. "Keep it. Kyan will be pissed if he knows you paid."

I glance over my shoulder to see Kyan looking over at us. He's watching to see if Dane is going to take my money. "Alright. Well let me at least give you a tip. I won't take no for an answer." Dropping a ten dollar bill on the bar, I quickly turn and walk away before Dane can try to give it back. Kyan may not let me pay for drinks, but tipping is something that I *always* do.

Setting my glass down on the nearby table, I pull my small leather jacket off and drape it over a chair. "Does this mean I get to outdrink you and outplay you in pool tonight? It's a good thing I don't work tomorrow."

That earns a small snicker from Kyan as he rubs the blue chalk on the end of a cue stick before holding it out for me. "Are you trying to challenge me, Ms. . . . ?" He raises an eyebrow in question.

"Reynolds," I say with confidence. "And yes. I've just spent my whole day moving into this amazing building with my lazy best friend that barely lifted a finger the entire time. I'm feeling pretty damn powerful right now."

Taking a drink of his beer, he grabs for his own cue stick now and rubs some chalk on the tip. Getting prepared, he sets his stick down and runs his hands through the thickness of his brown hair, before picking up his stick again. "Good thing neither one of us will have far to go after this." He pulls the triangle off the balls before motioning for me to break. "I've had a long night at the gym so I'll be drinking quite a few of these."

I let out an amused laugh while walking around the table. "You don't scare me, big guy." I pat his chest as I walk by. "Oh wow."

"Wow what?"

I look up from leaning over the table. "I've just never felt such a firm chest before. That's all. You must work *really* hard in the gym. I'm wanting to look into a gym myself."

"I do." He flashes a confident smile. "And that's perfect, because there's a gym down the road. *Wilder Fitness.* They have the best personal trainers." His voice and body language oozes straight up sexiness and confidence whenever he speaks.

I really don't blame him. He has the right to be.

"Alright. I'll look into that in the morning. As long as I don't decide to sleep all day." I take my shot and smile as two solids sink into a pocket. "Sweet. I'm solids." I smile up at him, proudly.

One hour later and we're both onto our seventh beer. He actually thought I was kidding when I said I was going to keep up with him, but I definitely wasn't. He's already asked me about five times to take a break and have some water, afraid that I'll get sick.

I was raised by a man. A single man. I was raised tough and I don't back down. That's why I can be so damn stubborn.

"Nope." I lean over the table, but can't get close enough to the cue ball. "I'm good," I laugh, feeling a bit silly from my buzz. "I got this." I struggle on my tippy toes.

Out of nowhere, I feel his hands grip my hips and push me up onto the pool table. "Here," he says in my ear, causing my breath to quicken from his closeness. "Let me help you beat me." His arm wraps around my waist to keep me steady as I aim my stick and shoot. Too bad his closeness was more of a distraction than help.

"Now that's not even right." I end up hitting the side of the ball and screwing up my shot completely. "How is that even possible? I'm so good at pool. I swear." I sit up straight on my knees and end up grabbing onto his arm as my head spins.

"Whoa." He grips me tightly, moves the balls, and helps me lay down on the top of the pool table. "I think you've proved your point, Calla."

Placing both of his arms on either sides of my waist, he leans close and smiles down at me as I begin to laugh.

"Alright . . . so I admit it, I'm not much of a drinker." I hiccup, causing Kyan to smile and brush my hair out of my face.

"I live the boring life of a wedding photographer. I don't get out much. Don't mind me." I laugh again, unable to stop myself.

"Alright. Let's get your beautiful ass to your apartment so you can sleep it off." He leans in closer until our lips are almost brushing. "And by the way . . . you won." He smirks. "I only had six beers. I was going to cut you off at this one." Pulling me up, he picks me up and places me over his shoulder, wrapping his arm tightly beneath my ass. "Let's go."

My head spins when he stands up straight, causing me to reach out for something to hold onto. My breath hitches in my throat when I realize that it's his muscular ass. It feels delicious through his workout pants and I feel myself grabbing on tighter.

I hear him let out a small growl as I squeeze it at the exact moment he starts walking me out of the bar and toward the front desk. Once we stop at the desk, he asks the young girl which room I live in.

I'm surprised that without hesitation she tells him. Shouldn't she be asking some sort of questions or something? Good thing he's not some maniac serial killer.

Wait . . .

I place my hands on his back and push up once we step into the elevator. "Are you a serial killer?"

He lets out an amused laugh before setting me down to my feet and pinning me against the wall to help me keep steady. He tilts his head. "No. Are you?"

"If I were?"

His eyes look down, stopping on my lips. "Then I'd be happy to die from the hands of the sexiest serial killer to walk this earth."

The elevator dings, causing us both to look over.

He bites his bottom lip again before wrapping his arm around my waist and walking me to my door.

"Your key?"

I start to panic. "Oh crap! It's in my wallet. I left it . . ."

He digs into his back pocket and pulls out my wallet. "I got you, babe."

Looking at me, he reaches in my wallet for my key. Then he closes my wallet and unlocks the door.

Before I can think, he has me in his arms again as he pushes the door open and starts walking inside. Next thing I know, I'm lying on my bed.

I sit up and watch as he sets my wallet on my dresser. "How do you know this is my room?"

He flashes a dimpled smile. "Because the door was opened. You said you had a roommate so I assumed the closed one was hers." He runs his hand through his hair. "Goodnight, Calla."

Then, just like that, he turns and walks away, leaving me grinning like a maniac. My head spins again and that's when I take it as my cue to shut up and sleep.

Kyan . . . the sexy guy with a gym bag and firm ass. Holy wet dreams . . .

Chapter Two

Kyan

CLOSING THE DOOR TO ROOM 629 behind me, I jog to the elevator when I notice Ryder holding it open for me.

"Hey, man." He pokes his head out of the elevator and looks down the hall as I step inside. After a second, he pulls his head back in and allows the door to close. "Did you just come from those hot chicks' apartment? The new ones?"

"Yeah," I say stiffly, already knowing what he's getting at. "And the blonde already has a boyfriend, so don't even bother."

The elevator comes to a stop and I walk out without another word. All Ryder is about is partying and sleeping with every chick that he finds to be hot in this building. I mean I'm down for some fun, but not with any and every girl I can find. There has to be something about her that's worth more than one fuck.

I may not know Calla, but the hour I spent with her is enough for me to want more of her. I don't do relationships, not anymore. I don't have the time nor have I had the desire to be tied down to one girl, but to be honest, if she wanted me to pleasure her I definitely wouldn't turn her away.

That tight little body of hers deserves every lick of pleasure that my tongue can give her. Being a bit of a bachelor, I've had the time and energy to learn a thing or two the normal guy wouldn't be comfortable with giving a woman, or either just doesn't know how.

Remembering that I left my gym bag at the bar, I stride down the hall, nodding to a few drunken women as they pass, eyeing me up.

Dane takes notice of me as soon as I enter the room and is quick to grab my bag and set it on the bar for me. "Here you go, boss man." Giving me a curious look, he slides me a shot of whiskey. "Is Calla cool? She seemed a bit out of it when you carried her out of here."

I give him a nod before grabbing my shot and tilting it back. "She's good. Looks like she doesn't get adventurous very often."

"I'm sure that will change soon. Just wait until Hunter gets back."

I pull out a twenty and throw it down for a tip. "Yeah, I'm sure Hunter will have his fun. He always does."

Grabbing my bag, I slide it over my shoulder and stand here, letting my thoughts get the best of me. I steel my jaw and give Dane a tight nod. "I'm out, man."

"See ya," he says as I walk away.

I ride the elevator up to the 10th floor, the very top, and open the door to room 1020. It feels so good to walk into my apartment, and the first thing I do is fall back into my leather chair and close my eyes, enjoying the peace and quiet.

My plan earlier tonight was to just stop by the bar for one quick beer and come back up to my apartment. Once I saw her—Calla—I knew that plan would change.

Hell . . . even the back of her head had me enthralled and wanting to see more. The way her long, thick, blonde hair laid resting on her slim back made me think about what it would be like to tangle my hands in it. Then, when she turned around and

I set sight on those big, emerald eyes, framed by a set of thick lashes and those shiny, plumps lips, my dick twitched.

As if I wasn't already intrigued, she opened that mouth of hers and I knew I had to stay. She was fun too, with an addictive personality. Calla is definitely a girl that I want to get close to, but not too close; never too close, and I always have ways of making sure that never happens.

Laying my head back, I take a deep breath and slowly release it when I feel my phone vibrate in my pocket. I already know who would be calling this late on a Friday night.

I answer my phone. "Damn you, Hunter. It's been a long night."

I hear his annoying laugh before he finally speaks, "Oh calm your dick, big bro. It can't be that bad."

I let the events of the last week run through my head and then picture all the ways that I can choke the life out of Hunter when he gets back from his vacation. "Just make sure you're back by next Friday, Hunter. No more extending this shit. Got it."

"Already have my ticket booked. Anyways," he stops to talk to some chick that is saying his name in one of those annoying ways that makes you wish you were deaf. "I was calling to let you know that I haven't partied myself to death . . . yet. Gotta go take care of Hillary. See ya, dic . . ."

He's still talking when I hang up. I really don't want to listen to his voice right now. It's even more annoying when I'm pissed at him.

Closing my eyes, my thoughts instantly go back to Calla. I haven't seen a woman with such natural beauty in a long time, possibly even ever. Most women pay to obtain the beauty that she probably doesn't even know she possesses. Maybe I need to show her just how damn beautiful she is.

I scan down her body mentally, picturing the way her tight, little plump ass looked in those skinny jeans. I feel the beginning of an erection and a bad case of blue balls coming on.

Damn . . .

I haven't had blue balls in a long time. Probably not since I was like sixteen. I never had any problems after that in that department.

Undoing my jeans and zipper, I push my hand underneath the waistband enough to lower my briefs and jeans down to my thighs to allow my thick erection to break free.

Biting my bottom lip, I grab ahold of my shaft and start to stroke my cock to my filthy thoughts of Calla riding my face. I can picture me wrapping my hands in the bottom of her long hair and pulling as she rides it slow and hard, letting me taste her until her juices wet my tongue.

Surprisingly, it doesn't take long before I feel a slight tug in my balls, followed by a loud moan through my lips as my orgasm rides through me, my cum squirting into the palm of my other fisted hand, or at least mostly. It's hard to contain my loads.

"Shit." Tugging my shirt off, I clean up my mess, wash up quickly, and pass the fuck out in my bed, partially satisfied and still hard.

Fuck me . . .

Chapter Three

Calla

STUPID, STUPID BEER. I HATE you. I sit up slowly, holding my head in my hands. "It's so bright!" I cover my eyes. "Why is it so bright in here?"

I hear the sound of Tori's footsteps before I hear my bedroom door open. "What the hell? Why are you screaming and waking up the whole apartment? Brad and I are still sleeping. Shush your mouth in here and put up your curtains for crying out loud. It's bright as fuck in here."

"Screw you too, you sucky friend," I mumble as she walks out of my room, slamming the door behind her.

I moan and groan to myself while crawling back under my blanket and hiding my face. "I'm so hungry." I internally cry while remembering that all of our stuff is stilled packed up. The only things we managed to unpack were bedding and some bathroom stuff.

Rolling over, I allow myself to fall off the bed, wrapped up in my blankets. I lay here for a few minutes before mustering up the energy to slowly make my way into the bathroom and splash some water on my face.

Standing here, looking at my reflection, my thoughts change to the bar last night. Sexy guy. Nice face, nice lips, nice . . . everything, and with a gym bag.

"The gym," I mutter.

I remember everything about the night. It was really the last beer that put me over the edge. Then my head started spinning and I got really tired.

"Shit. So much for a good first impression." I grip onto the sink and roll my eyes. "Laying on the pool table. Nice job," I groan.

The best thing I can do right now is run a nice, warm shower and relax as the water massages my skin. That sounds so good right now.

I stand here for a second, trying to remember where I stuck the box of towels and shampoo. The only thing I unpacked last night when first arriving was a small box filled with a few rolls of toilet paper, our toothbrushes, and tampons. Just in case . . .

I spend the next twenty minutes searching for the stuff I need for a shower and a fresh set of clothing. I have a few pairs of yoga pants and some tank tops that will be appropriate for the gym, so I settle on those before turning on the shower water.

The water comes out hard and fast. "Oh thank goodness!" I squeal while quickly stripping myself of my clothing. The last apartment had shitty water pressure, making it impossible to enjoy a damn shower. I've never been so excited over a shower in my entire life.

Closing my eyes, I moan as I step under the water and slide the glass door shut behind me. I turn and let the water beat down on my upper back. It hurts, but feels good at the same time. I stand here, enjoying the feel of the hot water as the room starts to fill with steam.

I'm in the shower for over thirty minutes, never wanting to get out. I just feel so refreshed and relaxed. I could seriously stay in here all day; that is until Tori starts pounding on the door and yelling at me to get out. Damn whore. She always ruins everything, but I love her. Did I mention that?

"Fine!" I scream from the shower. "Calm your tits and give me two minutes."

When I walk out of the bathroom Tori is standing there doing a pee dance. She practically growls at me before rushing into the bathroom. She doesn't even bother to close the door.

"Oh my God." She lets out a satisfied sigh. "I had to pee so bad."

She flushes and walks out of the bathroom, watching me as I hold my towel together. "When did you get home last night?" She kicks a few boxes on her way to the kitchen. "You were still gone when we fell asleep and you didn't answer your phone. I sent Brad downstairs to find you and he said you were playing pool with some guy."

I try to hide my smile as she fights her way into a box and pulls out a glass. "Yeah," I say nonchalantly, trying to conceal my excitement. "I don't think I was gone that long. Maybe two hours or less."

Twirling my wet hair in my hand, I turn for my bedroom.

"Whoa. That's it?" I hear the faucet turn off before the sound of her feet on the wood flooring. "You were playing pool with some guy and I don't even get any details?" She stops in front of me. "Was he cute? Did you kiss? What did he smell like? I mean . . . these details are very important."

"Yes, no, and very delicious." I side step around Tori and stop in my doorway. "I'm going down the street to check out that gym: *Wilder Fitness.* Do you want to come? I think I'm finally going to look into a personal trainer."

"Sounds tempting—having a personal trainer at least. Working out . . . not so much. I'll pass." She smiles devilishly when Brad calls her name from the bedroom. "I have all the workout I need, chica."

"Thank goodness. I'm leaving then."

I STAND OUTSIDE OF *WILDER Fitness,* looking through the glass at all of the people working out. Practically all of the equipment is in use and it's only ten in the morning. That's insane. I've never seen such a busy gym before.

I suddenly feel a little nauseous. I don't mind other people seeing me work out, but when you have to stand around and wait for equipment, you start to get noticed. *What if I use something wrong? That wouldn't be embarrassing in the slightest.*

I do a weird little shake, letting my nerves roll through me. "Just think—firm thighs and butt. Firm thighs . . . and butt."

"Good pep talk."

I freeze to the familiar sound of the deep voice behind me. *Kyan . . . Mr. Sexy as sin.*

He reaches for the door and pulls it open, before smiling and nodding for me to enter. "Glad to see that you're awake. Come on."

I smile, remembering how lousy I felt this morning before my shower. "It was a struggle. I won't lie. But I made it."

I walk under his arm and into the gym. All I can hear are the sounds of heavy breathing and music. My nose instantly gets assaulted with the smell of sweat, but then gets hit with the sexy smell of Kyan as he grabs my hand and pulls me along behind him.

I can't help but to notice random girls watching with smug looks as we pass by until we're out of sight, stopping at a door in the back.

I'm thinking he's about to knock, until suddenly, he's pulling out a key, sliding it into the keyhole. He pushes the door open, flips on the light, and motions for me to follow him inside.

He points at the chair in front of the big, black desk. "Take a seat, Ms. Reynolds."

I look around me, checking out the office, before taking a seat. I guess this means that he's a manager or something. "So you're a manager here? Is that why you recommended this gym? Very good marketing skills." I look at him and smile as he drops his gym bag behind the desk and takes a seat in the other chair.

He flashes me a cocky grin that has me crossing my legs behind the desk. "Of course not." He leans back and runs a hand through his sexy, tousled hair. "I'm the owner." He sits up straight. "I was just coming back from grabbing a bite to eat. Good timing, I guess."

I'm silent as he starts pulling up screens on his computer.

"Do you have an idea of how many sessions you're looking for?"

I chew the inside of my cheek in thought. My eyes widen when out of nowhere I feel his hand grab my chin as he massages a thumb over my cheek to stop me.

"There's no need to be nervous. No one at my gym is here to judge. You'll get to see that. Just relax."

I look at his hand as he releases my chin and goes back to the computer. "I don't know. I didn't really think about it," I admit. "What do you recommend?"

His gaze sets on mine and his jaw slightly flexes. "I think you're already sexy as hell. I don't think you *need* personal training, so don't get me wrong when I recommend this. I'm only here to please you, Ms. Reynolds." His eyes lower down the front of my body, him not making an effort to hide it. "I have a special going on right now."

He glances back at the computer and changes something. "It's originally twenty- four hundred, but I'm going to put you in for twelve hundred. That gives you forty- eight sessions and you get charged weekly, not all at once."

"Wait. Wow." I shake my head at his generosity, not sure if it's polite to accept it. I barely even know him. "That's really not necessary, Kyan. This is your business. Don't short yourself for me."

"I'm not shorting myself. Trust me." His powerful gaze captures my eyes as he continues. "I don't offer this to many people. Actually, this is the first time. Don't turn me down, because when it comes to you, I feel the need to give and satisfy."

I swallow hard from his words, now starting to feel flushed. I shake the top of my tank top. "It's getting hot in here. Is the heat on or is it just me?"

Kyan laughs while standing up. "It's just you, Calla." He walks over to me and grabs my hand, helping me to my feet. "I'm also waiving your membership fee. It's been a while since I've felt so . . . *giving.*" He turns behind him and reaches for a measuring tape. "Stand up straight."

He stands directly in front of me, his body just inches from mine as he runs his hands down my arms, before lifting them. "Stay still while I take your measurements. Just relax your body."

I nod my head, biting my bottom lip as I take notice of the goose bumps rising on my arms and legs as he carefully takes my measurements and marks them down. When finished, he hands me some kind of device to hold so that he can measure my body fat or something.

We both sit back down afterwards as he types up a bunch

of information.

"You do wedding photography," he states."

I nod my head as I reply. "Yeah. I've been doing it since graduation."

"Have you ever done any other kind of photography?" He watches me curiously, waiting for an answer.

"Well yeah. Nothing too different. A few birthday parties and one time I got asked to photograph a bachelorette party." I lift an eyebrow at the memory. "That was pretty interesting."

"I want you to photograph me."

My head shoots up. "What do you mean? Are you getting married or . . . ?"

I let the question hang in the air while he stands up and walks around the desk, stopping at the front. Leaning against it, he crosses his thick arms and looks down at me. "No." He lets out a small laugh. "One of my gym members is a local author and she asked me to be on her cover. I need someone to photograph the shoot."

I catch myself checking out his body as I let his words sink in. The thought of us alone as I take his picture is oddly arousing. "Alright," I say simply. "I can do that, but for free. I won't let you pay me."

"I won't be," he says. "The author pays for the shoot. She's already given me all the details and ideas that she has in her head. She's too busy to be there, so it will just be the two of us."

"Okay. Yeah. We can shoot in my apartment."

He shakes his head. "We'll do it in mine." He looks down at my tight clothing as I stand up. "And wear something comfortable. You might find yourself in some odd positions."

I laugh a little at his choice of words. "I'm sure I have something." I pause for a second while wondering if he's going to assign me with a female or male trainer. I'm kind of hoping for a female so there's less awkwardness. "What's my trainer's name?"

"Kyan Wilder." A smirk appears on his face as I watch him. "Come."

I'd love to . . .

He opens the door and starts walking out, so I follow behind him. He stops to encourage a few men that seem to keep their eyes on me as we pass. We finally stop in front of another door and he opens it for me to walk in. The lights are already on, so he just closes the door behind us and *locks it.*

Walking over to a small stereo, he turns it on and starts talking. "I'm going to begin with an easy workout to get you started. The last thing I want to do is scare you off on the first day." He smiles at me and I swear one of his dimples melts me on the spot.

He steps up behind me and places his thumbs in between my shoulder blades, massaging my back. "Spread your legs a little," he whispers in my ear. I do as he says. "Perfect." His breath brushes my neck, causing a shiver to run up my spine. "Do twenty squats. Keep your shoulders straight."

I face toward the wall of mirrors and do as he says. I can't help but to notice him biting his bottom lip as he watches me. It's almost as if he's tasting me with his intense stare.

"Watch yourself when you move, Calla, not me. See how you control your body."

I pull my eyes away from him and watch myself in the mirror, feeling slightly hot from the way he demands control.

He takes me through four different exercises, doing counts of twenty each, three different times, before he switches it up and ends it with jumping rope for five minutes and holding a plank for one minute.

By the time he is done with me I'm covered in sweat and

my legs are so wobbly that I feel like I'm going to walk into a wall and smash my face into the mirror. *What a sight that would be . . .*

I'm standing here, trying to catch my breath, when Kyan appears in front of me with a water bottle. "Drink."

I grab it from him and begin to drink it. I notice him watching me with a smile when I pull the bottle away. Yes I'm aware of the water that is covering the front of my face and chest, but is it polite to make it known that you notice? I just worked my ass off. I'm hot.

With a confidence in his step, he closes the distance between us and grabs the back of my neck, looking down into my eyes. "You look beyond sexy when you're wet, Calla. I would love to lick every last drop of water from your body." He runs his tongue over his bottom lip and hovers his mouth above mine. "Are you free tomorrow for the shoot?"

Fighting to catch my breath and not fall over, I shake my head. "No. I have a gig tomorrow. I'm not free till Monday."

"Perfect," he says. "I'll see you then."

Then, just like that, he unlocks the door and walks away, leaving me breathless and desiring his touch.

Stupid gym bag guy . . .

Chapter Four

Kyan

I HAD TO WALK AWAY when I did. I was more than tempted to kiss her and lick the mixture of water and sweat from her neck and breasts. I can't do that yet, not until I know that she's willing to keep things solely on a sexual level. I want to please her . . . not hurt her. Until then, I'll keep my hands off of her beautiful body.

Mitch, one of my personal trainers, comes into my office as I'm closing down my computer and grabbing for my things. He watches me carefully before speaking. "Are you done for the day?"

I look up as I shove Calla's paperwork into my bag. "Yeah. I think you and Erica have it. You have three employees coming in at noon and another three at four. You know where to reach me."

He follows me out of my office as I close it behind me and lock it. "Were you doing personal training back there?"

"Yeah." My eyes linger toward the back room to see Calla walking through the gym, checking out the equipment. I feel bad for not taking the time to show her around, but I can't be around her too much until I can touch her. It's too painful, physically.

"You don't do personal training," Mitch says with a lopsided grin. "Are you sure you don't want me to take over?"

I stop walking and look him straight in the eyes. "No. She's my first and only client. Don't question my decisions."

He takes a step back. "Sorry, boss. I didn't mean any harm. Just trying to be friendly."

I let out a grunt and walk away. *Friendly my ass. You want to fuck her just like I do.* The difference in him and I is that I am willing to pleasure her in ways that this young dick hasn't even had a chance to learn. I fuck for her pleasure. That's what drives me. This fucker is nineteen and has slept with half of his trainees, only being sure to get himself off I'm sure.

Setting my Harley in my sights, I secure my bag, before mounting her and pulling my helmet on. A nice, long ride is what I need right now before I find myself standing outside of her door, rock hard, and ready to hold her on my shoulders so she can mount my face.

The way her pussy looked in those tight little yoga pants didn't get past me, and I could smell her body as she started to sweat. That beautiful place between her legs was wet all right, and I have a feeling that it wasn't only due to her workout.

Monday . . . I'm going to have her taste all over me.

Chapter Five

Calla

I STILL CAN'T GET OVER my workout session with Kyan on Saturday. His amber eyes watched me as if he wanted to taste me and I loved the way his sexy lips spoke to me. His voice is so strong and seductive. *Doesn't he realize what he does to a woman?*

I haven't seen or spoken to him since. My phone goes off and a text from an unknown number comes through; maybe that's about to change. The words make it clear that Kyan has taken down my number from the front desk. You would think that in an upscale building like this they would be stricter on the privacy of their tenants.

> *Kyan: I'll see you in 3 hours. Apartment 1020. Wear something comfortable or nothing at all. ;)*

I stare at my phone for a second before responding. I said I was free to photograph today. How does he know I'm not busy for the next four or five hours? He's demanding, and oddly I find it refreshing and sexy.

> *Me: Very funny. I'll definitely be wearing something . . . and I may or may not be free at seven. You'll know if I show up.*

I get an immediate response as if he was already typing out his message before I even replied.

Kyan: I've got everything you need. Just bring your camera.

Not bothering to respond, I smile to myself as I set my phone down on the living room floor and continue to unpack the box I'm working on. He's so certain that I'm showing up, so there is use in fighting it. Three hours will give me enough time to finish unpacking, eat, and take a quick shower.

Tori and I spent most of yesterday at the *Miller Wedding*, but came home late and got a lot of unpacking done. Luckily, we're down to about four more boxes. Thank goodness!

"Hey woman!" I yell.

Something comes flying at me from the kitchen. "Do you really have to yell? I'm like ten feet away."

I look beside me at the spatula now lying on the floor. I pick it up and toss it back in the kitchen. "I'm starving. What do you want to do for dinner tonight? We can go downstairs to the bar. The food smelt pretty good when I went there on Friday night."

"Sounds good to me. I just want some really good chicken wings. I don't really care where they're from."

I pull the last DVD from the box and shove it onto the shelf. "Mmm. That sounds really good right now." I push the empty box aside and go to join Tori in the kitchen. "What's left in here? If I don't eat within the next hour I will cry. I'm that hungry."

Reaching above her to place some plates in the cabinet, she tilts her head back and turns it to the left of her. "That box right there. It's full of all the stupid pans. That's the last box for the kitchen."

"Good. Let's just finish the kitchen, go eat, and then we'll finish the other boxes before I take off for my shoot."

Tori freezes from reaching into the box and spins on her heels to look at me. I may have forgotten to tell her that little detail. "What shoot?"

I shrug my shoulders at her while ripping the tape off the box of pans. "Kyan . . . the guy I met at the bar on Friday."

"Yeah." She pushes my shoulder. "Go on."

Ignoring the fact that she's standing directly over my shoulder like a damn creeper, I start putting the pans away. "He's my personal trainer. A local author asked him to be on her book cover and he asked me to photograph him."

"What!" She shrieks. "You get to photograph this cute, good smelling guy that you didn't kiss and you didn't even bother to tell me about it?" She slaps me in the back of the head with a whisk.

I whip my head in her direction with my mouth open in shock. "You, hooker. You just hit me."

She hits me again, but on the shoulder this time. "And you kept something from me. We're even."

"You think at least," I say barely above a whisper.

She looks down at me now holding a wooden spoon. "What was that?"

I grin up at her. "Nothing. Let's hurry up so we can eat. Being hungry is brewing a love/hate relationship with you."

"I second that," she mumbles. "So stop talking so much and work."

I TOSS MYSELF DOWN ONTO my bed with a full tummy.

Dane was downstairs at the bar and he recommended the garlic wings and garlic wedges. HOLY shit they were delicious! I don't know who the chef was, but I so would have kissed him if he showed himself. He didn't, so I settled with kissing Dane on the cheek since he was *only* the one that suggested them.

Rolling over flat on my stomach, I look down at my phone to check the time. We stayed down at the bar longer than expected. I have less than forty-five minutes before I have to be at Kyan's.

His words, *wear something comfortable,* run through my head as I stand in front of my closet. Maybe I should just surprise him and go with his second option: *nothing at all.*

I laugh at the thought, trying to picture his face if I were to show up like that. I wonder what would happen. Would he throw me across his bed and give me the best fucking of my life, or would he laugh at me and send me home to put some clothes on? The second thought gives me a sinking feeling in my stomach.

That would be humiliating.

Standing in the shower, I start to picture the first option: him coming to his door and let's say . . . shirtless. Yeah, that sounds good. He comes to his door shirtless, wearing only a pair of snug fitting jeans.

Closing my eyes, I start to touch myself, slowly massaging my clit. I'm surprised at how sensitive it feels already.

He notices me standing in his doorway naked, so he wraps an arm around my waist and pulls me into his apartment . . . or maybe he just tosses me over his shoulder like a caveman. He does seem a bit on the rough side.

I start to rub myself harder and faster as more thoughts and scenarios of Kyan run through my head. It doesn't take long before my legs become shaky and I find myself holding onto the wall, panting as my orgasm washes through me.

"Oh wow. Oh wow," I repeat, breathless.

A stupid grin tugs at my lips as I lean my head against the shower wall. It's been a while since I've experienced an orgasm that quick. It sometimes can take up to twenty minutes. That's no fun.

I jump when I hear the toilet flush. "Shit!" I poke my head out of the shower door to Tori washing her hands. "What the hell? How long have you been in here?"

She smiles while drying her hands on the pink and brown towel. "Oh wow! Oh wow!"

Grunting, I turn the shower water off. "Haven't you ever heard of privacy?" I can't help but to smile at Tori's face as she makes an O with her mouth. "Laugh all you want, but it felt good as shit; probably even better than those half-assed ones that Brad gives you."

Her face turns serious. "Shit. I told you about those?"

Reaching for my towel, I laugh and nod my head. "Yup! All I have to do is give you a bottle of wine and you like to talk." I get in her face and start moving my hand as if it is her mouth. "Talk. Talk. Talk. I'd be careful if I were you."

I push her with my hip and walk past her. "Maybe Brad should get his lazy tongue checked out. Aren't there some kind of tongue exercises he can do for crying out loud?"

"I wish," she mumbles.

"I need to get ready for my photography date." I grin, and walk away, leaving her probably hating Brad and his unsatisfying tongue. Strangely, that leaves me satisfied.

Holding my camera, I run my hand down the front of my white shirt. He said to dress comfortably, so I did. I settled on a pair of cut off denim shorts, a loose shirt, and a pair of my worn out Chucks. I have my thick hair pulled to the side in a loose ponytail. Swallowing, I knock.

It only takes a few seconds before Kyan is standing before me looking even sexier than the last couple times I have seen him. *How is that even possible? He's magic, that's how. I wonder what kind of spells he can work with his tongue . . .*

He's dressed in a black V-neck shirt that hugs his broad chest so perfectly that I start to believe that shirt was made specifically for him. Lowering my gaze, my eyes widen as they take in the way his thick legs look hugged in his dark, form-fitting jeans.

He rests his arm above him in the doorway and I unknowingly lift an eyebrow as his shirt slightly lifts, revealing a thin happy trail, leading into the top of his black boxer briefs.

"Ms. Reynolds," he says with a knowing smirk. "Looks like you were free after all." He steps away from the doorway, allowing me to enter.

I take a few seconds to look around as he closes and *locks* the door behind us. Setting my camera down onto the marble counter top, I walk over to the black, plush couch and push down on a cushion. "Oohhh . . ."

He gives me an amused smile. "It feels even better when you lay on it . . . especially when you're naked, in the dark, just closing your eyes and getting lost in your thoughts." He looks up to meet my eyes. "I find myself doing that a lot after a long, hard day at work."

I suck in a breath and try to hide my silly grin as I picture just *that* in my head. "I can imagine," I say.

"I'm sure you can." He walks into the kitchen and reaches above him in the cabinet. "I'm going to have a beer while we work. Will wine work for you? I'm not sure if beer is your thing." I hear a hint of humor in his voice, so I make a face at him before nodding my head.

When he walks back into the living room, he sets a glass of red wine down onto his coffee table before handing me a piece of printed paper.

"Those are her visions for the shoot. I already know what she wants me to wear so as long as you can pull off the rest . . ." He pauses to take a swig of his beer. "Then everything is all good."

I swallow hard as my eyes scroll over the words on the paper. I've *never,* and I mean as in *ever* done a photo shoot so exposed and personal before. According to this piece of paper I'll be photographing him in two different places: a white room, and in his bed. What he will be wearing . . . now that is his little secret and for me to find out, but from the covers I've seen floating around these days; I'm going to guess it's going to leave me sweating my ass off and wiping drool from my chin.

Reaching for my glass of wine, I smile nervously and lift it to my lips. I take a long swig before wiping my mouth off. *At least it's not drool.* "I'm ready when you are."

Kyan watches me over his beer as he tilts it back. He sets the bottle down next to my glass. "We'll start with the white wall." He nods to the open door to our right. "I have a tripod set up and all the necessary equipment that you'll need to get the right angles. I wanted to make it as easy on you as possible."

"Perfect," I say, trying to sound as professional as possible. "I'll go set up my camera while you get ready."

Quickly, I reach for my camera and hurry into the white room. There's nothing in here except for camera equipment. I hear Kyan enter the room, but I focus on turning on my camera and getting it placed in the tripod.

I hear him shuffling around and getting ready. When I look up again, I see him pulling his shirt over his head and tossing it aside. Of course my eyes have a mind of their own and I end up checking him out in slow motion as he stands there shirtless, his tight muscles flexing as he leans against the wall, waiting for me to pull my shit together.

I've never seen a man with such a beautiful body in my life. The last time I have been this fascinated with a man's body was in high school. *Hunter . . .* That was one fine man. Now, it's with my neighbor and damn personal trainer.

I may have released a little moan when his V of muscles appeared as he tugged his jeans down to where he wanted them.

I will not run over there and lick them. I will not run over there and lick them . . .

I shake my thoughts off and start giving him orders. I am pleased with every single shot that I take. That never happens. Kyan is just so naturally sexy that it takes no effort for him to pose, making it easier to feel professional. I quickly get into it.

I tell him to bring his left arm to the right side of his head and look at me through his arm, and he does. The way his body is placed, all of the right muscles flexed and on display are fucking flawless.

"Perfect," I say a little breathy. "Now stand with your back facing the wall and bend your right arm over your head. He flexes his jaw and gives me a seductive look as I snap a few pictures. "That's so good, Kyan. You're a natural."

We do a few more poses before I decide that we're ready for the next session of the shoot. We've been working on the white wall shoot for nearly forty minutes now and we have well over a hundred good shots.

Kyan is watching me with a lazy smirk as I look down at my camera. "I guess the next spot is in my bedroom. Not many girls get invited in there." He tugs on the end of my ponytail as his eyes roam over my body. "Good thing you dressed comfortably. You need to be flexible for this part."

I watch the way his ass and back muscles move as he exits the room. "Holy shit," I say to myself. I pull my shirt away from my chest as I get an instant rush of heat through my body. He does this on purpose; uses the perfect words to make a girl sweat bullets. He's sexy, smooth, and successful; the perfect blend of trouble.

I stop in his doorway and watch him as he undoes his jeans and tugs at his zipper. His eyes meet mine and stay there, as he drops his jeans and kicks them aside. I can't help but to take notice of his thick thighs and how they flex whenever he moves.

Drool . . . don't expose yourself now.

He walks over to stand in front of me and reaches for my camera, setting it down on the foot of his bed. It sinks into the thick, white blanket and we both watch it before locking eyes again.

"Show me how you want my boxers." Grabbing my arms, he places my hands on the top of his briefs.

"Excuse me?"

He takes my fingers and hooks them into the front of his black briefs. "Pull them down to where you want them. Show me."

This is too much power. Too much power is *never* a good thing. I gently tug them down a bit, exposing the top of his hipbones.

He laughs. "Are you uncomfortable with me being in my boxers?" He pulls me toward him. "Let's fix that."

Before I know it he's on his knees, tugging my shorts down my legs.

I instantly get embarrassed. "What are you doing?" He grabs my hips and lifts me as he kicks his foot out and pushes my shorts across the floor.

"There. Now we're both in our underwear. Better?"

I look down at my black, lacy panties, before looking up to see that he's biting his bottom lip. Again, he always seems to do that when he shows interest.

I feel silly so I start to laugh. "Are you serious?"

He reaches for my hands again and practically shoves them into the top of his briefs. "Dead serious." He flashes his dimples. "Now take control and show me how you want my boxers."

The power behind his demand feeds me and I find myself tugging his black briefs down until the top of his thick shaft is exposed, along with the top part of his muscular ass.

' He looks down and lifts an eyebrow. "Better." He hands me my camera before he walks around the side of the bed and tugs the huge blanket off, leaving nothing but a black, silk sheet.

I feel oddly confident standing here in my underwear about to photograph America's sexiest bachelor. I'm not sure if this is a temporary confidence, but it feels good. I'm having fun. I find myself kicking my shoes aside and jumping onto his bed while trying to balance my camera.

He smiles up at me as he lies down on his back and adjusts the sheet so that it's between his legs. Without my direction, he places one hand behind his head and waits for me to start snapping pictures. It seems with each click of the button that his briefs start to get lower and lower, exposing more of his body.

Playing it smooth, he flips over onto his stomach. He lowers his briefs until the top half of his ass is exposed. His ass is so round and firm that all I want to do is bite it. My breathing picks up as he slides one arm under his pillow and looks up with a seductive look in his eyes.

He must notice my change in breathing, because his eyes meet mine and suddenly he sits up and gets on his knees below me. I'm standing on his bed and he's just looking up at me with the sexiest face I've ever seen.

His question surprises me. "Have you ever thought about fucking me?"

My saliva thick, I swallow, and let out a nervous laugh. "What?"

He reaches for my camera and pulls it out of my hand, before tossing it beside him. Then he grips onto my hips and looks up at me. "Have. You. Ever. Thought. About. *Fucking.* Me?" He grips my hips harder when I don't answer him. "Tell me the truth. Please don't ever lie to me."

My words come out before I can stop them. "Yes. I mean. I have once or twice . . ."

He wets his lips, his eyes locked on mine. "Do you think you could have sex with me without expecting more and getting emotionally involved?" He massages the spot right below my belly while removing my ponytail with his other hand. "Can I pleasure you and know that you won't expect anything more? No ties. You're welcome to fuck who you please and same goes for me. I just want to taste you so fucking bad."

I think about it for a second and the thought alone has me clenching. I give him a slight nod and close my eyes as his hands move a little lower.

"Say it, Calla. Tell me that you want me to pleasure you and I will make you come so hard that I'll have to carry you to your apartment."

I open my eyes and look down at his sexy face. His lips. . . . oh God. I want them on me. "I want you to pleasure me, Kyan. I can handle it."

Without hesitation, he lifts me, placing my legs around his neck. I shudder when I feel his stiff tongue run up, between the folds of my pussy. Even through the fabric it has me squirming.

I squeeze his face with my thighs as one of his hands

tangles into the back of my hair and his tongue pushes my panties aside.

Oh my God . . . he has such a strong tongue.

I feel his tongue slide up my bare pussy, tasting me as his moan vibrates up to my clit.

My thighs squeeze his face tighter as I moan out, already close to reaching orgasm. I want this so bad that it won't take long.

Leaning me backwards, he lays me down on my back and massages his thumb over my pussy before tugging my panties down my legs. "I want you to ride my face. I've been thinking about tasting you for days."

He dives between my legs and softly nibbles on my clit before moving his tongue around in small circles to ease the pain. He grips my thighs hard while working his tongue so perfectly that I scream out as I feel myself start to clench.

"I'm so close. Kyan . . . Kyan . . ." I pant.

He smiles up at me before removing my shirt and pulling me with him until I'm straddling his face. His thick stubble brushes against my pussy, giving me a sense of pain and pleasure at the same time. "Ride my fucking face until I taste your release on my tongue. I want every fucking last drop."

His hands slide under my ass and squeeze as I rock my hips, slow and hard, moaning as his tongue licks every inch of my pussy. His tongue slides in and out a few times as he pushes me down into him harder and harder with each rock of my hips.

Then, he slides his tongue out of me and swirls it around my clit before sucking it into his sweet mouth.

"Oh my God . . . Kyan!" I scream and grip onto his thick hair as my orgasm rolls through me, and he's right . . . he doesn't stop. He keeps licking until I fall still from feeling so weak and drained.

I feel his hands run up my back before he lifts me off his face and sets me down beside him.

"Holy fuck," he runs his tongue over his lips, tasting what's left of me on his mouth. "That was so fucking good. Next time I want my cock in that tight little pussy of yours, Calla. I want to feel you as you squeeze me."

My whole body shivers from his words and the thought of him fucking me. Hearing him say it only confirms how badly I really do want it. I never expected to have a *fuck buddy,* but I have to admit that I love the sound of it. At least I get to touch this man.

"I hope we got enough shots for the cover," I say out of breath.

I hear him laugh before he reaches down and adjusts his thick erection. "We have more than enough. Trust me."

We lay here for a few minutes just enjoying the silence, and I can't help but to feel my stomach sink at the thought that I didn't even get to feel his lips on mine. They're just so soft and sexy, but I don't want to bring it up. I have no idea how this all works.

Without even an ounce of awkwardness, Kyan helps me get dressed and walks me to his door.

He hands me my camera, but pulls it away as I reach for it. Before I know it he has me pressed up against the wall, his mouth crushing against mine.

His free hand reaches up and squeezes my chin as his tongue runs along the seam of my lips, before swirling around my tongue as I open up for him.

This man knows how to use his tongue. He's definitely no half-assed Brad. It's as if he takes pride in being able to use his tongue for the pleasure of others.

The perfect man . . .

He pulls away and smiles against my lips while handing me my camera for real this time. "Thanks for the shoot." He shoves some cash into the front pocket of my shorts. "This is from Olivia. Don't try to give it back. Her email is in there as well." He backs away from me and opens the door. "Meet me at the gym Thursday night at eight. I have a special training session set up."

"Special?" I question, with a lift of my brow. "I'll see you there." I walk out and laugh, not bothering to turn back to look at him. I seriously have no idea how I should feel right now, but I feel good. Too damn good.

I don't hear his door close until I step onto the elevator. The doors close behind me and I immediately fall against the wall, breathing heavily.

"Holy shit! Is this even okay?" My vagina sure in the hell doesn't care. That's for damn sure.

I find myself in slight panic mode before I calm myself down and give myself a little pep talk, reassuring myself that it's perfectly natural for two grown people to fuck just for pleasure. It's something that happens every day, just not with a man as sinfully sexy as Kyan.

This is something most girls can only dream of . . .

Chapter Six

Calla

I HEAR TORI'S ANNOYING VOICE yelling in my ear. "Hello! Are you in there?"

I elbow her in the tit. "Don't yell in my ear. Yes, I'm in here." I gesture around the dimly lit room at the dancing couples and overdone decorations. I'm surrounded by red and gold. "I'm just ready for this damn reception to end." I look down at my cell phone to see that it's already seven thirty. I'm supposed to meet Kyan at the gym by eight and this party doesn't look close to ending soon. "It's been going on since three. Aren't they tired yet? My finger's going to fall off if I click that button one more damn time."

Tori raises a brow, bored. "Tell me about it. Not only is it the longest reception in history, but it's also boring as shit. Where's the booze and Funyuns? Seriously though. These people have poor taste in refreshments."

Okay, so she might be over exaggerating a bit on this being the *longest* reception in history, but it sure feels like it. I'm getting so antsy that I can't even think straight.

It's already bad enough that my mind has been on Kyan for about eighty percent of the night, and now that it's getting close to seeing him again, I'm beginning to feel impatient.

I start walking around just snapping a bunch of pictures in hopes that if I get to a certain number of shots that I can just leave. The newlyweds are slow dancing to about their fiftieth song and everyone else is now watching in wonder. I guess it could be that the couple is in their sixties. I guess them being out this late is sort of a big party for them, even when there isn't any *booze* or *Funyuns.*

Joining in the clapping, I smile at Mrs. Crawford as the couple finally leaves the dance floor. She gives me a slight head nod and walks in my direction.

"You looked beautiful out there, Mrs. Crawford. And so happy. Congratulations."

She gently tugs my arm and pulls me close to her ear so I can hear her speak over the music. "You and your friend did a lovely job, but I think we've kept you kiddos late enough. Go home and enjoy your night."

Yes! Yes! Yes!

I smile small and tilt my head. "Thank you for having us. Please tell Mr. Crawford that we'll have the disk ready in a week," I say, while trying to stay calm and not too overly excited about finally getting out of here.

She nods once and waves before walking away to join her husband at the table. She's been away for less than two minutes and it already looks as if he misses her. *Isn't that something?*

Tori lets out a long, relieved breath next to my ear. "Thank *fucking* God." She links her arm through mine, and then starts walking me toward one of the tripods. "Let's get the hell out of here before I start to wrinkle just from looking at all of these old people. There's old people everywhere and it's seriously starting to freak me out."

Tori and I pack up our equipment faster than we've ever packed up at a wedding before. By the time we get in my jeep, my cell phone already reads two past eight.

"Shit, I need to hurry." I shove my key into the ignition and hurriedly pull out of the parking lot. It's about a ten-minute drive to downtown Chicago and I still have to change into my new workout gear.

Tori looks up from typing on her phone as I impatiently tap the steering wheel when the car in front of us slows down. "Don't get your titties all twisted. Why the rush?"

I scrunch my forehead and concentrate hard on the road. "I'm late for my training session at the gym. It's rude to be late. I don't want to leave a bad impression."

"I bet you don't, hussy." I hear her typing fast on her phone to whom I'm sure is to be Brad. "I bet Mr. Sexy is ready to work you. I may just need to go to the gym with you sometime so I can get a look of this fine piece of man meat."

I laugh at her choice of words. "I'm sure we'll run into him in the building sometime and you can meet this *man meat.* He does live on the tenth floor," I remind her. "No need to twist your arm to get you in the gym."

"True," she says uncaringly. "Maybe he'll be at the bar or something and you can introduce us. Then I can see who has my roomie all flustered and fluffin' the muffin."

I stop a little too abruptly at the stoplight, my face turning beet red. I haven't mentioned the events of Monday night to her yet so she really has no idea just how turned on and *flustered* he truly has me. I'm not really sure how to explain, so I won't. Not yet. "You talk a lot. You know that?"

"Oh you're just embarrassed because some guy finally has your lady parts working. There hasn't been anyone in over two years. You really need to get out more."

I grind my teeth at her reminder. "It's been by choice. I'm just not looking to date right now. When I am, I will look."

I FIND MYSELF RUSHING TO the gym door as soon as I jump out of my jeep. I have to catch myself from face planting when my feet hit the blacktop. That's how fast my feet are shuffling right now.

I'm already thirty minutes late and I was in such a hurry that I didn't even bother stopping to send Kyan a message. I have no idea if he'll be upset and I really don't want him to think that I forgot about our session.

When I look around me, the parking lot is empty; all except for an expensive looking motorcycle parked close to the building. It confuses me, causing my steps to slow. "Shit! Please don't be closed."

I place my hand on the handle and pull, expecting it to be locked, but it easily opens, surprising me. A surge of hope rushes through me at the thought that I'll at least get a chance to explain. I just hope the bike outside is his.

Walking inside, I look around me, but don't see anyone else in the gym. One of the tanning room lights are on as if someone may have recently gotten out, but besides that, it's just rows of empty equipment.

Once I get closer to the back, I notice Kyan's office door is open, so I jog a little to get there faster, not wanting him to have to wait any longer than he already has.

I poke my head inside to see Kyan leaning against his desk, dressed in a black, sleeveless shirt and a pair of gray shorts. He looks sweaty and out of breath, as if he's just finished with his own workout.

He looks up as he takes notice of me. "Calla." He smiles.

"Hey." I watch him as he pushes away from his desk and

walks over to stand in front of me. He doesn't say anything. His eyes just check out my breasts as they slowly rise and fall. "Why is the gym empty? Am I too late? I got held up with a wedding. I'm really sorry."

Another small smile appears on his face as he grabs the strap of my purse and slides it down my shoulder. "We can leave this under my desk." He places it on his chair and pushes it back under his desk. "And you're not too late. You're *never* too late, Calla. I have all night. I'm here for you."

Placing one hand on the small of my back, he guides me out of his office and over toward the treadmills. "The gym's empty because not a lot of members workout between eight and nine. It's one of the quietest time slots that are still early enough for you to come. You seemed a little nervous around everyone on Saturday, so I wanted to make sure you're comfortable." We stop in front of a treadmill and he motions for me to step on it. "Let's get you warmed up a bit first."

"Okay." He presses the start button and punches in my weight. Surprisingly he's only about four pounds off. I give him a shocked look since he never weighed me on Saturday. "How did you know? I . . . was that a guess or did you steal a sneak peek of my license that night at the bar?"

He studies me as I start walking with a confused expression stuck on my face. "I'm pretty good when it comes to a woman's body." He lets out the sexiest laugh to ever grace my hearing. "Looking at your body, it's pretty easy to figure out. I was close, huh?" He lifts an eyebrow, waiting for my confirmation.

"Well yeah. You're close." I start moving faster as Kyan ups the speed. "Pretty impressive."

Without another word, Kyan smirks and leans against the treadmill right next to the one I'm on, watching me intently and clearly enjoying the show.

By the time our session is over, I'm insanely sweaty and out of breath. He showed me a few of the different machines and had me rotate between those and carrying some weight across the room. I stand here for a moment with my hands on my hips, watching as he watches me. "I'm so tired," I say softly. "This is the most intense workout I've ever done."

"We're not done yet."

My eyes widen. "What do you mean we're not done? You've been working me for the last forty minutes."

He comes up behind me and presses his body against mine. An instant rush of heat spreads throughout my body as he brushes his bottom lip over my ear and gently laughs. "I'm not done working you yet. There's plenty more I want to do."

My breathing picks up. I watch his eyes on me as he circles around to stand in front of me. His eyes linger down to my chest that is quickly rising and falling, as I stand here imagining his mouth and hands all over me.

Wetting his lips, he steps closer and reaches out, tangling both his hands into the back of my hair as he whispers, "Just sex?"

My eyes lower to his lips and I find myself nodding. "Just sex," I whisper back.

As soon as the words leave my lips, Kyan picks me up, wraps my legs around his waist, and kisses me so hard the air gets knocked out of me.

His hands wrap tighter in my hair and his breathing picks up as he starts walking with me in his arms.

Before I know it, we're in the shower room. I don't even notice Kyan reaching to turn the water on until we're both standing below the water getting wet.

I jump a little from the surprise, but easily fall back into kissing him when he tugs on my bottom lip with his teeth.

"Fuck, your mouth tastes so good." Leaning my head back, I moan as his lips run over the front of my neck as his hands tightly grip my ass. "I need to be inside you."

Setting me down to my feet, he yanks his shirt over his head before quickly grabbing my shirt and ripping it open. I stand here panting and soaking wet, as I watch the water fall down his face and slowly drip over his luscious lips.

The muscles in his arms flex as he reaches for me again, slamming me up against the wall behind me. He moves with such intensity that I don't know what to do, so I just stand here on shaky legs, waiting for him to take me.

The bra is the next to go and he doesn't waste any time before dropping to his knees in the water and tearing my black pants and panties down all in one pull.

I hear a small growl deep in his chest as he looks up at me from the ground. "You're so fucking beautiful." He spreads my legs before gripping my ass cheeks and pulling them apart, sliding a finger up the crack of my ass. "I want to be sure to taste every last inch of this body before we're through. I want to pleasure you in every fucking way possible."

He runs his tongue up my thigh, stopping just below my pussy. I bang my head against the wall, not wanting him to stop. I need this so bad right now. It's been so damn long.

I let out a moan as his thumb runs over my clit, causing my whole body to jerk under his touch. "I love seeing you squirm, Calla. Pleasuring you is all I want to do. I'm going to do things to you that no one else has."

Pulling away, he reaches into the changing section of the shower and sticks his hand into a black duffel bag, before pulling out a condom. Biting his bottom lip, he pulls his shorts down, stroking his hand over his thick erection, as he stands there now completely nude.

Holy fuck! That looks like it hurts.

I start to get nervous as he steps closer, stroking himself a few more times before ripping the wrapper open with his teeth and tossing it aside. "Turn around," he demands. Without hesitation I turn around. "Bend over and place your hands on the mat."

Swallowing, I look down at the mat before bending forward and placing my hands in front of me. His hands grip my hips and lift until they align with his. "Wrap your legs around my waist."

I wrap my legs around his waist, holding myself off the ground with my hands, and squeeze when I feel his dick poking me. I've never had anyone put me in this position and I have to admit that it has me so turned on. It has my arms shaking, but I'm willing to hold on for as long as I can. He runs his hand over my ass in circles before gently slapping it. "So perfect."

Holding my balance, I suck in a deep breath and moan when I feel the tip of his dick enter me. "Mmm . . ." I grip onto the mat and whimper under my breath as he pushes it deeper, adjusting me to his size. After a few seconds he's all the way in, and I have to admit that it hurts more than it ever has before with someone inside of me. Even though he's not moving yet, just the thought of having him inside of me has me already beginning to clench.

"You okay?" He asks. Hold on."

I nod my head once.

"Fuck, you feel so good."

He pulls out of me, and quickly thrusts back in, almost causing me to lose my balance, but I hold my arms steady, not wanting this to end too quickly. I want this. I want him in me.

Both of his hands dig deeper into my hips as he continues

in a steady rhythm, burying himself to the hilt with each thrust. We both moan out as he goes faster and harder, slapping the water between our bodies. It's loud and hot; so damn hot.

His hips sway and he grinds himself into me so good that my legs hurt from me squeezing him so tightly. I've never felt such intense pleasure just from a man being inside me. This feels so good that it's almost unbearable. I want to scream, but I stop myself, afraid that if someone comes in that they'll hear me.

He pounds into me and stops. "Squeeze my dick with your tight little pussy, Calla." He pulls out and thrusts back into me again. I scream out as my arms almost give out. "Fuck, you take my dick so good."

He lifts my legs higher and begins fucking me so fast that I lose my breath with each time that he slams into me. After a few seconds, I feel my orgasm starting to build and it's so sensitive that I almost can't take the buildup.

"I'm coming, Kyan . . ." I squeeze the mat and cry out as he slams into me over and over again, giving me the most intense orgasm that I've ever had. "Holy shit! Oh God! Oh God!" He lifts me up during mid orgasm to give my arms a rest.

"Fuck yes. Squeeze my cock, baby." He waits for my body to stop clenching before he sets me back down and drops to his knees behind me. "You okay?"

I nod my head as he turns me around so that I'm facing him. "Yes," I say breathlessly. "So good."

"Good . . . because I'm not done." He pulls me up to my feet and stands directly on the mat. "I need to come now." Picking me up, he wraps my legs around his waist and grabs my ass with both hands.

I throw my head back and moan as he lifts me and sets me down on his dick. Grabbing onto him for dear life, I bury my head in his neck and bite him as he pounds into me over and over again.

He moans out and grips my waist tighter as he gets close to reaching his own orgasm. I'm surprised that just by knowing that he's about to explode has me clenching around him once again.

"Oh fuck!" I feel his dick throb inside me as my orgasm rolls through me for a second time. One of his arms wraps around my neck as we both breathe heavily, our bodies spent. His breath covers my lips and I feel him smile against me. "This is the best workout I've had, and I'll definitely be wanting more sessions like this."

I smile before sucking his bottom lip into my mouth and biting it. This causes his eyes to lock with mine, before he turns his gaze and carefully sets me down.

We're both standing here under the water for a few seconds before Kyan speaks, breaking the silence. "Why don't you get dressed while I clean up and then I'll follow you home? You did bring a change of clothes, right?"

"Yeah," I say softly. "Sounds good."

Kyan appears from the shower room about fifteen minutes later, dressed in a pair of jeans and a gray shirt.

He smiles at me and grabs my hand. "Let's go."

I ABOUT FELL OVER AND fainted when I watched Kyan mount his motorcycle when we left the gym. His sexiness level is now off the chart and I'm not sure how much more of it I can handle. I mean, a woman can only handle so much, right?

I feel his hand rest on the bottom of my back as we enter

the apartment building and walk toward the front desk.

The blonde girl at the desk smiles at me and then looks to Kyan. "Hi, Mr. Wilder. You have some messages and a reminder from your brother that he'll be back tomorrow morning."

Kyan reaches for the index cards as the girl hands them out for him. "Thank you, Ashley." His hand goes lower, stopping on my ass and I have to fight the gasp that almost escapes my lips. "Anything else I should know?"

Ashley nods toward me. "Would you like me to tell you at a different . . ."

"She's fine," he says, cutting her off. "Tell me now."

She clears her throat and gives me a forced smile. "It looks like Ryder Owens is late on rent again this month and Mrs. Moore is going to pay tomorrow when her check comes in."

He grinds his jaw. "Tell Mrs. Moore not to worry. She can pay when she can, and I'll deal with Ryder myself."

Kyan brings his hand back up to my lower back and gives a little pressure to let me know that he's ready to start walking.

I wait until we get in the elevator to ask him a pretty obvious question after the conversation I just witnessed a few minutes ago.

"Do you own this place too?"

"Yeah," he says, still looking a little worked up about this Ryder guy. "I bought it from my father a few years ago and then opened the gym up with my brother."

"Wow!" I smile as the elevator dings. "Someone's a pretty busy man."

He walks out onto the sixth floor and pulls me along beside him. "I'm a very busy man. Too busy sometimes."

Once we get in front of my door, he presses my back against it and rubs his thumb over my throat. His eyes meet mine. "I need you to promise that you'll use protection with others. Every. Single. Time."

"I've always used protection. I'm safe when it comes to sex."

He gives me a satisfied nod. "Me too. Always." His hand wraps in the back of my hair and his eyes lower to my lips. "Goodnight, Calla." He leans in and kisses me on the side of the mouth. "I'll text you later about our next session."

I swallow and nod my head. "Goodnight, *Mr. Wilder.*"

He flashes me a sexy grin before taking off toward the elevator. I immediately unlock the door and push it open, disappearing inside.

"Ouch! Ouch! Ouch!"

I've been keeping that in for a while. I'm sore; so sore. All over. Especially between my legs, but I didn't want him to know that he hurt me, because I don't want him to take it easy on me next time. I want this just as much as him.

Maybe even more . . .

Chapter Seven

Kyan

I STEP INTO THE ELEVATOR with Calla's taste still tingling on my lips from the gym. I was so close to kissing her on the mouth when I said goodnight at her door that I had to stop myself before going through with it.

Kissing isn't something that I take lightly. I usually keep kissing in the bedroom to keep that safe line between dating and just having unattached sex, but her lips feel and taste so damn good that I'm so close to saying fuck it and blurring those lines.

"Fuck!" I step out of the elevator and onto the tenth floor. My eyes wander down the hall to Hunter's door before I shove my key into my lock and let myself inside.

Hunter gets back tomorrow and finally I'll have a little help around here. I'm so exhausted by the time I get home each night that thinking is physically painful, and I know for a fact now that since I've had sex with Calla I'm going to be doing a hell of a lot more thinking.

Being inside her felt a lot better than I expected. I had to try my hardest not to come before I got her off first. I always get the woman off first, but with her I was almost selfish.

I pick up my phone and think about sending her a text, but then toss it aside, deciding against it.

Instead, I strip down to my boxers and go to bed, thinking about how and when I'm going to fuck Calla again.

It definitely has to be soon . . .

Calla

INSTEAD OF GOING TO BED I find myself behind the computer, pulling up photos of Kyan from the shoot on Monday. I've been so busy editing other photos that I haven't had much time to go through the cover shoot and I need to have the edited pictures sent to Olivia in two days.

With each picture that I click on, I find myself smiling at how well we worked as a team that day, and I guess maybe just a *little* at the way he made me ride his face. Okay, so a lot, a whole lot.

Wedding photography is enjoyable, it's what I'm used to, but this . . . this is a whole new level of fun. I can definitely see myself looking into doing more personal shoots, especially if it's with Kyan.

I turn my head to the side when I hear Tori come out of her room. She nods her head at the computer and walks to the kitchen. "Whatcha looking at?"

I wait until she's done pouring a glass of juice before answering her. "My photo shoot with Kyan."

Tori's slippers rub against the wooden floor, bringing attention as she scurries my way. "Yes please. I need to see this."

I bring my hands up to cover her eyes as she bends down

to get a look. "Yes please? I never asked you to come look." I laugh as she slaps my hands away and looks down at the screen.

"Oh damn!" She looks closer at the photo of Kyan under his sheets, looking up at me—the camera. "Did you photo shop this delicious man or was he just blessed with every good genes that God made?"

Shaking my head, I laugh and click through a few more pictures, giving her a taste of what I've been tasting . . . literally. "No actually. This is my first time even looking through them. This is all him. *Man meat* all in his sexiness wonder."

She leans against the computer desk and sips her juice, keeping her eyes glued to the screen. "Well damn . . . this man could do *anything* that he wanted with my body. I'd pay him just to lick my big toe. No lie."

Without thinking, I say my thoughts aloud. "Well he's definitely good with his tongue; *so* good."

I get shoved into the desk as she jumps up to her feet. "Oh my God! What did you just say?"

"Nothing." I lie. "I was just thinking." I can't hide the smirk that takes over my lips. Who would be able to?

"Girl. If I was doing *anything* with a man this sexy, denying it would be the last thing I would be doing." She slowly starts walking to her room. "You think about that and then tell me all the details in the morning. All the details. Every single one. I'm going to sleep. Brad wore me out and not in a good way."

I shut down my computer and think about what she just said. A huge smile takes over my face and I feel like a giddy kid. She's right. I should be screaming from the rooftops right now. This is the best deal I've ever been hit with.

I just had sex with the hottest guy to walk this planet, he

gave me not one but two orgasms tonight, and I don't plan on giving him up any time soon.

My muffin has never been so happy . . .

Chapter Eight

Calla

I SPENT THE ENTIRE DAY editing wedding shoots with Tori while she continued to drive me bonkers and question my sanity. I'll admit, the day actually went by surprisingly fast, but as soon as she took off with Brad for the night I knew that I needed to come downstairs for a drink or two. Anyone would need to after spending an entire day with her.

I've been sitting here at the bar, talking to Dane for the last hour now. The guy works practically every night and apparently it's by choice. He only takes one night off a week to spend with his family. He has a fiancé named Kylie and a three-year-old daughter named Melissa.

Kyan promised him first pick of the schedule and hours each week before the other four bartenders, and although Kyan has offered him a raise so he can work fewer hours, Dane said that he wanted to be sure he earned that raise first. Kyan's good to him and I can see just by talking to Dane how much that truly means to him. It shows how caring Kyan truly is.

Dane gets pulled away from our chitchat once the bar starts to pick up, so I find myself sitting here alone, twirling my phone in my hand. With just one click of a finger and a short elevator ride, I could be upstairs in Kyan's apartment, held up against one of his walls. I have to admit that the thought has crossed my mind many times today.

My mind is tempting me. It's very tempting, but the more that I think about it, the more I start to tell myself that this isn't a relationship. I can't just start calling and texting him anytime that I want. That scares guys away. I've learned that and I don't want to do that with him. What happened in the gym last night was the best sex of my life, and there's no way I'm screwing that up by getting any feelings involved. The more you call someone—see someone—fuck someone . . . the more you want them and lines get blurred. I'm not ready for that.

I stiffen, with my straw between my lips, when I feel soft breathing close to my ear. My eyes close on instinct, waiting for a voice, and expecting it to be Kyan, but it's not.

"*Someone* fucked up by not calling you." The voice is deep, but not as deep as Kyan's, yet it sounds vaguely familiar.

I let out a nervous laugh and stop myself from twirling my phone. "The type of relationship we have doesn't require calling," I admit.

Setting my phone down, I turn around in my stool and bring my eyes up to see a very attractive man. At closer look, I realize that he also looks familiar.

My heart does this crazy little twist and a small dance when I realize that it's *Hunter.* It's been over five years since I have seen him and he looks even better than he did in high school. I had a *huge* and I do mean *huge* crush on him back in my senior year. I just never had the guts to approach him.

"Hunter?" I ask with a smile.

He tilts his head and gives me a closer look. "Well damn . . . Calla." Smiling, he reaches for my hand and pulls me up to my feet. Surprising me, he wraps me in a hug before pulling away and looking me over. "You look really good. It's been a long time."

I allow my eyes to linger over him, checking out his long, lean body dressed in a pair of old faded jeans and a black button down shirt with the sleeves rolled up to his elbows. He's not muscular in a huge way, but more of in a toned way. It's very sexy, and I have to admit I wouldn't mind seeing that body without clothes on. I've imagined it plenty of times in the past. Bringing my eyes back up, I stop on his blue eyes and smile as he brings a hand up, running it through his smooth, brown hair.

"You look really . . . hot." I shake my head and laugh at my admission. "Sorry." I hold up my drink. "I've been wanting to say that for a long time, and I guess this pretty purple drink helped with that."

He lets out a little chuckle before pulling out the stool next to me and taking a seat. His lips pull up into a cocky smile as he waves Dane over, while still watching me. "Hey, Dane. I'll take one of what she's having. Might as well just go ahead and make three now and save some time."

Dane leans over the bar giving us both a strange look. "Sure thing, Hunter."

"So . . ." He leans over and takes a sip of my drink, smiling when he's done. "That's actually not too bad. A little fruity, but you know . . . it works."

"Yeah," I say. "Just a little bit, but fruity is what I asked for, so Dane is doing an awesome job. Plus, it's kind of embarrassing sitting at the bar, getting drunk alone. I'm not prepared to be on the receiving end of laughter tonight."

Dane quickly places our drinks in front of us, says enjoy, and scurries off to help a few girls calling him over.

"I agree," he says with a laugh.

I wanted so badly to talk to Hunter back in high school, but having him here in front of me now, I'm unsure of what to say.

I've seriously dreamt of moments like this with him, so now is not the time to sound like a huge loser. "So . . . you live here?" I ask.

Please say yes. Please say yes.

He takes a swig of his drink while nodding his head. "On the tenth floor."

My heart stops at the mention of the tenth floor. It immediately brings my thoughts back to Kyan. A small part of me feels guilty that I'm sitting here all flustered, talking to Hunter, but the other part quickly reminds me that Kyan wants no attachments. He's made that clear more than once. Talking to Hunter is probably good for the both of us.

"You?" He questions, pulling me out of my thoughts.

I pull my lips away from my straw as I point up. "On the sixth floor." I smile. "Just moved in last week and I absolutely love it here. It's beautiful."

His eyes widen as he looks me up and down, making my cheeks flush red. "Glad to hear that. That means we'll definitely run in to each other again. I definitely don't mind that."

"This is weird," I admit.

"Why's that?" He leans in close and pulls my chin up to look at him. My eyes set on his full lips as he speaks again. "That we live in the same building?"

I let out a small laugh, not even believing what I'm finally about to admit. I've kept this from him for six years. "I kind of had this small crush on you in high school. Okay, so maybe a *huge* crush, but I was always too chicken shit to approach you."

He smiles big, making my heart speed up. "I had no idea." He releases my chin and takes another drink, watching me over the rim. "I had a thing for you too."

I look up at him, eyebrows scrunched in disbelief. He's messing with me now. Either that or I've had one too many purple drinks. "You don't have to say that to make me feel better, you know?"

He shakes his head and laughs as if he's surprised that I think he's joking. "I'm not. I seriously thought you were incredibly *hot*. I almost asked you to dance with me at a party once, but I saw you with some guy so I didn't bother."

I feel my heart crush at the mention of Jordan. That's something that I don't want to think about. It's been over two years since I have let his name even cross my thoughts. I need to steer this in a different direction and fast, before I lose my shit.

"Yeah . . . well you should have asked anyways."

He watches me closely as I unknowingly start to down my drink faster. "Maybe I should have," he says. "Someone a little thirsty tonight?"

I look down at my drink, with my straw hanging between my lips. It's already halfway gone and I had just ordered it right before Hunter showed up. I release my straw and sit up straight. "Just a little bit. It's been a long day." I smile and bite my bottom lip as he watches me. "What?"

He leans in closer and brushes my hair behind my ear, before leaning in and whispering, "I was thinking maybe I should dance with you now to make up for it."

I feel his thumb brush below my ear, and without thinking, I lean my head back and close my eyes, leaning into his touch. "Oh yeah," I say softly.

I feel the slight brush of his lips below my ear before he speaks again. "Yeah. You look so sexy right now, and since no one is *supposed* to call you . . ." He grabs my hand and helps me to my feet. "Then I think it's up to me to show you a good time."

Releasing my drink, I let him walk me out to the dance floor where there's a small group of people dancing. A few eyes land on us, but no one says a word as we find a spacious area.

Without hesitation, he links an arm around my waist and pulls me against him. His body grinds against mine in a way that sends a shiver throughout my body. He definitely knows how to work his hips, and I have to admit that it turns me on.

I feel a small breath escape me at the realization that I would have died to be this close to him in high school and now here I am, up close and very personal.

Being in his arms right now gives me a small rush, and I have to admit that I like that he doesn't seem shy with me. He moves my body in ways that he wants without hesitation, not worrying if it's crossing a line or not. It's intoxicating.

"Is this weird?" He whispers next to my ear. "The way I move your body with mine . . . because I've honestly wanted to do this for years."

Spreading my legs with his knee, he places his leg between mine and grips the back of my neck, slightly dipping me backwards. He grinds his hips a few times, causing my heart to skip a beat from our closeness.

I grip onto the front of his shirt and move my hips with his when I feel one of his hands squeeze the bottom of my left ass cheek. Our bodies are as close as possible and I can feel the thickness of his erection poking me, driving me insanely mad.

All I can keep thinking is *Hunter James. This is the Hunter from high school.* Feeling his hardness against me is something I never thought would happen. I feel like a blushing little schoolgirl right now.

His hand squeezes my ass tighter, causing me to let out a small moan as his lips slowly caress my neck. "I want to taste your lips so fucking bad, Calla." He shamelessly grinds his hips into me, making his erection very clear. "See what being close to you does to me?"

I let out a nervous breath when he grabs the back of my head and without hesitation, presses his lips to mine, tasting me as if he's been waiting forever for this moment.

When his tongue slips into my mouth to swirl around mine, I moan into his mouth and grip onto his shirt for support. His sudden kiss steals my breath away. No joke. I actually couldn't breathe for a second when I felt the brush of his tongue on my bottom lip. My heart is beating insanely fast and my thoughts are going fucking crazy as I stand here kissing him back.

It feels so damn good to finally be kissing Hunter, but at the same time has me thinking about how I was just kissing Kyan yesterday, and not to mention, having the best sex of my life.

We both pull away from the kiss, breathing heavily, and a satisfied smile forms on Hunter's lips as he watches my expression. "Fuck . . . that felt nice; better than I'd imagined."

"Yeah," I admit, before licking my lips. "Really . . . really nice."

We stand here for a moment before Hunter pulls his phone from his pocket. "Shit. My brother has been texting me." He presses his lips to mine one more time before reaching down into my pocket and pulling out my phone. He punches his number into it and hands it back to me. "I was supposed to be at my brother's over an hour ago and he's definitely not happy with my ass right now. The fucker is blowing up my phone." He points down at my cell. "Save my number. I want to hang out soon."

Swallowing, I look down at my phone before smiling up at him. "I think we can make that happen."

He smiles and starts backing away toward the bar. "I sure hope so, considering we only live four floors apart. Text me so I have your number." He turns away and whistles to get Dane's attention before tossing some money down onto the bar and rushing out of the bar.

Dane holds up the money and smiles over at me, letting me know that once again, my drinks are free.

Hunter James. The Hunter James. This is crazy . . . Oh wow.

Chapter Nine

Kyan

HUNTER BURSTS THROUGH MY DOOR wearing the biggest shit-eating grin I've ever seen on him. Apparently his ass was with a girl, *of course,* so he decided that catching up on his work wasn't as important. It's always the same with him.

He automatically goes to my fridge and pulls out a beer. "Damn. I really need to change my number." He tosses the cap in the garbage and leans against the kitchen island. "I could have been getting my dick sucked and you really would have ruined the mood with your texts."

I pull out a stool and straddle it. "And I could have been giving your job to someone more responsible than your ass." I lift a brow as he shrugs his shoulders. "Your dick can fucking wait until after business."

Hunter rolls his eyes while taking a swig of beer. "You really need to loosen up a bit and stop working so damn hard. Ever since that bitch fucked you over with Bryant, you've dedicated all your time to this fucking place and the gym. You're not even thirty yet and you do nothing but work your ass off. Both places are extremely well run, but you always want more. It's as if you're looking for ways to bury yourself in work and forget about everything else around you."

I flex my jaw at his words and reach into the fridge for my own beer now. I didn't call his ass to my apartment to discuss this shit. "Running both of these places are at the top of my priority list. What the fuck do you expect from me?" I toss my beer cap at him as he opens his mouth to speak. "Don't even fucking answer that, brother."

We both sit here in silence, sipping on our beers as I let his words repeat in my head. It's been three years, and every day my heart still feels as if it's being ripped from my chest repeatedly. Burying myself in work and not letting any attachments form has been my life since then.

That's exactly why I'll do anything I can to avoid falling for Calla. She's the most beautiful woman I have ever lain eyes on, and I can't even manage to be in the same room with her without wanting my hands all over her and pleasing her in every way that her body deserves.

Hunter smiles beside me as he pulls his phone from his pocket and punches in a quick text.

I nod down at his phone in his hand. "Your new girl for the week?"

He lets out a small groan and adjusts the crotch of his jeans. "This girl is *gorgeous.* She might just be the sexiest woman I have ever laid eyes on." He stands up and grabs two more beers out of the fridge. "I went downstairs for a few drinks and saw her sitting alone at the bar. When I approached her, I realized that she was a girl that I'd desperately wanted to sleep with in high school. She just seemed too good for me, plus she had a boyfriend at the time."

I let out a small laugh while finishing off my beer. "Too good for you? Nah. I doubt that, playboy."

He holds up his phone as it vibrates. "Yeah. You're right." He chuckles. "She's single now and apparently is open to unattached sex. It's a good opportunity for me to finally get to show her a good time and not have to worry about hurting her or getting tied up. Her body just screams sex, bro. I need to have her at least once, or a few times . . . you know."

I continue to drink my beer as my little brother's mouth *continues* to work as if I care about his endless fuck fests.

"And to make things better . . . she lives here." He jumps to his feet and runs a hand through his hair. "She just moved in on the sixth floor. Calla Reynolds. Fuck, she's so beautiful."

What the fuck did he just say?

My heart skips a beat and I spit out the drink of beer I've just taken. Well shit.

Hunter watches me carefully as I set my beer down onto the black marble. "Holy fuck. You're the one that's not *supposed* to call, aren't you?"

He starts pacing in front of me with a huge smile on his face. It's been a long time since I have shown any kind of interest in a woman and he's taking this time to enjoy the fact that I need to *fuck* just like every other man.

"Is big brother trying out unattached sex for once instead of the meet girl, fuck girl, and never see her again? You've been with her sexually more than once, haven't you?"

I let out a frustrated breath and steel my jaw. "There's no attachment. We're both free to *fuck* who we want, and there will be nothing more than me fucking her brains out and pleasuring her. I've made that very clear."

"So you won't care if I sleep with her then? We kissed downstairs, but I won't fuck her if you have feelings for her?" He tilts his head, waiting for my reply. "I guess our tastes aren't far apart after all."

A part of me wants to tell him to fuck off and leave her alone. That's exactly why I have to say this instead: "Nope.

You can do what you want with her, just don't fuck her over and make her feel used. You know how I feel about that shit, and if you're going to sleep with her . . ." I take a drink of my beer and force this last part out. "Wear a damn condom."

"You sure, bro?" He stands up as if he's about to leave. "Because I made plans with her tomorrow night. Now that I've seen her again, it's going to be hard to pass up this opportunity, so speak now or forever hold your peace."

I swallow hard while reminding myself that she's not mine to protect and that this is just casual sex. Nothing more. "Abso-fuckinglutely." I walk over to my door and hold it open. "Now go home and catch up on some fucking work before I kick your ass."

Raising an eyebrow, he smirks at me and walks out with an armful of my beers.

Fucking asshole.

I fall back on my couch and stare down at my cell. I get an urge in my chest to send Calla a message, but flip my phone over instead. Self-control is everything.

No attachments . . .

Chapter Ten

Calla

JUGGLING A FEW PAPERBAGS IN my arms, I impatiently wait for the elevator to arrive. Tori and I have already taken up a load each, and being restless I offered to go back downstairs for the last load. Of course Tori quickly agreed while falling in front of the TV with a beloved bag of her Funyuns, so while she's up there stuffing her face, I'm standing here cold and wet from the rain that decided to surprise me on my way back to the building.

"Finally," I say in celebration as the elevator opens up, allowing a couple of people to unload. The last person, a young guy with blonde hair, pauses to look back at me with a smile before hurrying off.

"Alright then." I step onto the elevator and just then, my eyes look up to see Kyan walking toward the elevator. He's dressed in a tailor made suit, looking so damn flawless that it causes my chest to ache as I fight for air. I'm so stunned that I can't even function enough to hold the door as it begins to close.

Right as it's about to shut, Kyan sticks his arm into the elevator, stopping it. Our eyes meet and he smiles while joining me inside.

"Let me help you with those."

Kyan quickly empties my arms of the groceries and watches me as the door closes, leaving us alone in this very small space. At least, right now it feels tiny; so damn tiny.

I smile back when he flashes me a dimpled smile. "Thank you. I was seriously tempted to just leave them outside for the homeless, but then I was afraid that my roommate would attack me if I came back empty handed. She's sort of obsessed with food." I lean against the wall as the elevator begins moving. "This is my second trip down and I wasn't expecting it to start pouring."

Kyan steps closer as I begin to slightly tremble from being cold and wet. He looks at me through a set of thick, wet lashes. "You have my number, Calla. Next time let me know and I'll take care of it."

I shake the water off my face and smile at his generosity. "Thank you. I'm not going to lie. It'd be nice to be dry right now."

His eyes lock with mine and I notice him slightly bite his bottom lip. Then, before I know it, his arm shoots out and stops the elevator.

His eyes linger from my eyes down to my lips before he drops the bags of groceries and pins me against the wall. His breath is sweet as it brushes against my lips, causing me to want to flick my tongue out and lick the outline of his lips. "You're so damn beautiful when you're wet. I think I'd prefer it if you were never dry."

His arm reaches around to grab the back of my right thigh and he raises it to his hip, stepping between my legs. He presses into me and I instantly feel clenching between my legs as his thickness pokes me through the thin material of my panties. Starting from the top of my chest, he brushes his lips up my neck, stopping just below my lips. One hand slips up my dress and I feel his finger slide between my folds.

"Kyan," I whisper, my body trembling from his closeness. "In the elevator? Aren't there cameras? I don't want anyone giving you a hard time if they see the security footage."

He turns away for a second as if he's thinking about it. His finger shoves inside me and his grip on my thigh tightens before he pulls away and wraps both of his hands into the back of my hair.

Leaning in, he whispers, "Sorry, it's hard for me to keep my hands off of you, especially when you're standing here wet with that dress clinging to your body." He runs his hand up the front of my neck before stepping away from me and fixing his suit, returning back to his professionalism.

I lean against the wall, trying to catch my breath while I stand here watching him breath heavily, as if he wants nothing more than to rip my clothes off and fuck me hard. That suit does nothing but make him look dangerously handsome and irresistible. A part of me wishes I would've just kept my damn mouth closed and let him take me again.

"It's okay," I say softly.

He reaches for the bags of groceries in one hand and quickly puts them back in the crook of one arm before starting the elevator again.

I stand here watching his side profile as he stares ahead at the door, as if he's about to lose a battle with his self-control.

The elevator dings and I quickly snap out of my thoughts as Kyan places his hand on the bottom of my back and guides me out of the elevator and to my door.

"Olivia sent me an email this morning telling me how much she loved the shoot. You did a great job," he says as I'm reaching for the door handle.

I smile up at him, feeling really damn good about that. "That's amazing. I'm really happy you gave me the opportunity to shoot the cover for her. I can't wait to see it."

I push the door open and step away to give him room to walk in.

I hear Tori begin to ask who he is until she sees me enter behind him.

"Holy shit." She places her hand to her heart as Kyan walks to the kitchen and sets the bags down on the counter. "I thought we were getting robbed by some crazy, sexy guy. I wasn't sure whether to run or be thankful."

Kyan and I both laugh at Tori as she stands there, staring at him like a lunatic.

"Tori." I clear my throat until she finally looks at me. "This is Kyan. Kyan this is my roomie and best friend, Tori."

"Nice to meet you, Tori." Kyan grins while reaching into one of the bags. "This must be the lazy roommate you mentioned," he says teasingly.

Tori looks at me, her hands on her hips. "You fucking twat. You told him I was lazy? Not everyone has the energy to be the damn energizer bunny like you. Some of us actually use our energy for better things like getting laid."

She tilts her head as my eyes look down toward the ground. *Fuck! Don't say anything. Don't say anything.*

"Wait . . ." *Double fuck!* "You're that guy that Calla did the photo-shoot with, right? The personal trainer guy?"

Kyan smiles while starting to put our groceries away. He surprisingly seems to know where most of it goes too. *Impressive.*

"You don't have to do that, Kyan." I rush into the kitchen, hoping to pause any awkward conversation that's about to start. Tori has always had a way of making conversations awkward.

Always. I grab the bread out of his hand and set it next to the bag. "Carrying these upstairs was enough. Trust me. I owe you."

"Why are you wet," Tori asks with a laugh. "It was completely dry when we brought the first load up."

I ignore her and smile up at Kyan. "Thank you. I can take care of these."

Stepping away from the counter, Kyan runs a hand through his wet hair, his muscles flexing, causing Tori and I to both stare like idiots. "Sure." He grips the back of my neck and softly presses his lips to the side of my mouth again. "I'll text you later about our next training session. I have a bunch of work to get done anyways."

I nod my head and smile as he walks over to Tori and reaches out to shake her hand. "Glad to have you in the building."

Tori tilts her head as she shakes his hand, making sure to grope his hand. "Sure," she says, confused. "Nice meeting you, gorgeous."

I hold my breath until the front door closes behind him.

"What did that mean, Calla?" Tori jumps up onto the counter to help me put groceries away. "Does he manage this damn building? That's insanely hot if he does."

"Not exactly." I throw a box of cereal into the cupboard above me, not really caring how it lands right now. "He owns it."

Tori's eyes widen as she blinks away the shock. "Holy shit! You're fucking the guy that owns this building?" She points at the floor. "This building? The one we're living in? The one we've been saving our asses off to get into? This expensive and very nice building?"

I turn toward her and toss a box of Pop-tarts at her head. "I never said I was sleeping with him."

She jumps down from the counter. "You don't have to

say it. I figured it out the other night when you came home all flushed while looking at his sexy pictures. Plus, he practically just kissed you."

"Yeah, but he didn't," I say, somewhat disappointed.

"More proof that you're fucking him." She grins while opening the fridge and tossing a bag of salad inside. "Men do that when they're trying to keep their hearts out of the mess that their dicks have them in. He's trying not to fall for you, honey. This is perfect for you. You're not ready to open your heart up again and he's not ready to give his. Perfect arrangement."

I stand here, leaning against the sink, letting her words sink in. If he's doing his part to keep himself from falling for me, then I need to do my part before I ruin everything.

Reaching into my jacket, I pull out my phone and read Hunter's message for the twentieth time since he sent it an hour ago.

Hunter: A friend of mine is having a small party tonight. Come with me.

I look up as Tori continues to ramble, but I'm not listening to a word she's saying. I can't. Biting my bottom lip, I reply to his message.

Me: I'm free for a few hours tonight. Pick me up around eightish?"

It only takes a few seconds for Hunter to reply, and when he does his words leave me slightly nervous and excited.

Hunter: I'll pick you up as soon as you'll allow me to. Wear something sexy ;)

Smiling from ear to ear, I set my phone down and continue putting away our groceries.

Please don't let me screw this up . . .

I'M JUST FINISHING UP MY makeup when I hear a knock on the front door. I instantly get nervous just knowing that Hunter is on the other side. A part of me wants to knock the door down just to get to him and the other part wants to hide before I end up getting myself into a complicated situation that I can't get myself out of. This still feels so surreal to me.

"I'm going to do this." I'm going to go out and enjoy this night with him as if I were still that damn teenaged girl just wanting one date with Hunter; one date, and now is my chance.

Tossing down my red lipstick, I quickly smooth out my tight little black dress before hurrying up to answer the door. Hunter told me to dress sexy, so I chose this dress, threw my hair into a loose, playful bun and slipped into my red heels. I definitely feel sexy, sexier than I have in a *long* time.

Pulling together a straight face, I open the door and smile at Hunter standing there, dressed to impress. He's wearing a black Henley shirt, a pair of black slacks, and some very slick dress shoes.

He whistles, as he looks my dress over. "Damn, Calla. You look incredibly sexy." He tugs on a piece of my loose hair. "Your hair looks hot up."

I hide my face, trying to avoid him noticing as it turns red. When I can gather myself, I turn back to him and let my cheesy grin take over. "Well, I've had this dress for a while and haven't had a chance to wear it yet." I point out his outfit. "And you look incredibly hot so . . . I guess we're a good match for the party."

"Absolutely," he says while reaching for my hand. "I can't wait to show off my date for the night. I'll just have to let the other guys know that you're off limits tonight." He smiles. "Let's go."

I step out of the apartment and close it behind me, before following Hunter down the hall. He stops in front of room 619 and lifts a brow as I look up at him. "We're here?" I ask with a slight laugh.

"Yup!" He pushes the door open and walks in first.

The first thing I spot is the blonde guy that I saw earlier leaving the elevator. He walks over and pounds fists with Hunter before walking over and grabbing my hand. "My new neighbor has arrived." He pulls me behind him and over to the kitchen where there's a crowd of people hanging out, drinking, and laughing. "Everyone!" The whole room gets quiet as he whistles. "This is my new neighbor and a friend of Hunter's, Calla."

I give an awkward wave as everyone says hi and starts to offer me drinks.

When I look behind me for Hunter, he's in the living room smiling at me as if he thinks I'm the sexiest girl in this room. Looking around, I definitely don't agree there.

The blonde guy smiles, looking me up and down, before passing me a drink. "Welcome to Ryder's house party, baby; always the best. Enjoy."

AFTER A COUPLE HOURS OF dancing and playing a few party games, Hunter and I find a quiet spot to relax. Somehow we end up getting on the subject of high school, so of course, Hunter brings up my little crush on him. I have to admit that it's a little embarrassing having him ask me all these questions.

I never thought that I'd ever be admitting this stuff to his face.

"So how long did you have a crush on me?" He pulls me down into his lap and wraps an arm around my waist. Being in Hunter James' lap has me smiling like a kid again.

"Do you really want to know?" He brushes his fingertips over my neck before kissing it. I guess that's a yes. "Since the end of junior year when I saw you playing catch in the cafeteria and the football accidently hit my friend Tori in the head. I crushed on you my whole senior year after that. "

He runs his hand up my thigh, stopping just below my panty line. "Oh yeah. She was pretty pissed." He kisses my neck again, but harder this time. "I remember you watching me. I smiled at you. You didn't get the hint?"

I shake my head and moan as he slips a finger under my panties. He lightly brushes it over my clit before pulling it away. "No," I say, my breathing erratic.

He pushes his hips into me, showing me that he's hard. "Are you getting the hint now?"

I suck in a deep breath as he bites the back of my neck, completely turned on. "Mmm . . . very much so."

"Good." He grabs my arm and stands us both up. "We need to go. Now."

Ryder throws his arms up when he notices us heading for the door. "Dude! Where are you guys going?"

Hunter opens the door and smiles back at him. "To have our own little party." He closes the door behind us before Ryder can manage to say anything else. "Is your roommate home," he asks impatiently.

I shake my head as he kisses my neck, leaving a tingling sensation as the air blows over the wet spots, giving me the chills. "No. She was leaving with Brad. She won't be home for a couple hours."

My heart is pounding so fast right now, and everything feels as if I'm in some sort of crazy fantasy. Kyan and now Hunter. I must be losing my mind.

Next thing I know, Hunter has my back pressed against my apartment door and he reaches into the front of my bra for my house key.

"How did you know my key was there?" I ask as he quickly unlocks the door.

He smiles and ushers for me to enter after he pushes the door open. "Where else would it be?"

As soon as we get inside, he slams the door shut and scoops me up, carrying me to the couch. He lays me down and is quick to lay himself between my legs. "I've been wanting to fuck you for six years now. You can imagine how crazy this might get."

His lips crush mine as he works on pulling my dress up my body and over my head. His hands are everywhere: my tits, my ass, and my neck, anywhere he can get them.

I throw my head back and close my eyes as his hand slithers down the front of my panties. This is all happening too soon and my thoughts are going into panic mode.

"Hunter," I breathe. "I'm sleeping with someone already. I'm not sure we should do this."

He pulls away from kissing my neck to look down at me. He grinds his hips into me and grabs the back of my neck, tilting my head to look at him. "Are you in a relationship?"

I shake my head.

He rubs his thumb over my bottom lip. "Does he want to be?"

My heart speeds up at the thought of Kyan not wanting an attachment to me. "Well no. He said we were both free to sleep with who we please."

Hunter grins down at me as if he just got exactly what he

was looking for. "There's your answer then." He sucks my bottom lip into his mouth before releasing it. "Live a little."

He's right. I want this so damn bad right now. At least my body is telling me that. How many more chances am I going to get to sleep with the one guy that I've crushed on for years and thought that I'd never have a chance with? How many? This is it. He's in my apartment, on my couch, and between my legs.

I grip the hair on the back of his head and crush my lips to his as he starts undressing himself above me. Before I know it we're both completely naked and he's pulling a condom out of his pants pocket.

He looks me in the eyes while ripping the condom packet open with his teeth and slipping it over his thick erection. I feel as if I can't breath as he pushes the tip of his penis to my entrance and pauses.

"I'm so fucking horny right now. I can't promise that I won't go too hard."

I suck my bottom lip into my mouth and moan as he shoves himself into me, not stopping until he's all the way in. He pauses for a second before pulling out and thrusting back into me.

His movements are rough and fast as he pushes one leg next to my head and grinds his hips.

"Oh fuck!" He grips the back of my head and slams into me harder, making the couch scoot slightly across the floor.

"Hunter!" I dig my nails into his back as he bites my bottom lip and continues to thrust inside of me. "Yes! Oh Yeah!"

"You like that?" He pulls out and pushes both my legs up as high as they can go before brushing the head of his penis over my clit. "You like that, huh? My big cock inside of you?" He rubs across my clit again. "You want it back inside of you?"

I nod my head and moan as he digs his nails into my thigh. "Yes," I say breathlessly. "I've wanted it for so damn long."

His eyes meet mine and he leans in to kiss me, before slamming back into me, taking me hard and fast. The couch is making so much noise that I'm afraid it's going to break.

Reaching down with one hand, he begins to rub his thumb over my clit. My thighs begin to tighten around him as my orgasm starts to build, but he shoves my legs back open and fucks me harder, until I've completely lost it and am shaking below him. Not even a few seconds later, he pulls out of me and strokes his hand over his dick as his own orgasm rocks through him.

"Fuck me!" He stands above me, still stroking himself while looking down at me. He smiles before leaning down and pressing a quick kiss to my lips. "Damn, you feel so good."

I look his body over and blush at his defined chest and abs. We got so lost in getting to the point that I didn't have a chance to fully check him out. He's absolutely gorgeous; yet, I can't help but to compare him to Kyan.

Kyan is just . . . I don't know what he is. He's almost unreal, as if he's not even human. He's painfully sexy in a way that makes you feel as if you're actually dreaming him up instead of looking at him in front of you.

Don't think about Kyan! What am I doing?

I shake off my thoughts and smile up at him. "Wow." I sit up, trying to catch my breath. "Did this really just happen?" I start reaching for my clothes to get dressed as Hunter walks his naked, sexy ass into the bathroom and flushes the condom down the toilet.

He walks back out. "I'm still wondering that myself. You do realize that all the guys in high school had a thing for you, right?"

I let out a laugh and push his chest after he pulls his shirt on. "Ha! Very funny, Hunter."

He grabs my hand and pulls me to my feet. "You think I'm joking?" He clenches his jaw before leaning in to kiss me. "About eighty percent of the football team talked about wanting a date with you, but everyone said you had higher standards. Everyone was pretty much too chicken shit to get turned down and ruin their reputation." He lets out a small laugh. "Me included."

I look down at our feet and do a silent scream of joy. Me? This girl? I pretty much thought that I was invisible most of high school until Jordan approached me. He was smart, sexy, and had his whole future planned out. I thought I was part of that future, but I was proven wrong; so wrong.

"I really don't know what to say about that. I never knew." I look up and smile as he backs away from me to zip his pants and button them.

"Well, now you do." He looks down at his watch before rubbing his thumb over my chin. "I really enjoyed this. We're just two adults having a little fun. If you start to feel like this is too much then we can stop. You're in charge here. Remember that." He quickly kisses my lips. "It's getting late and I have some more work to get done before my brother kicks my ass. He can be a little bossy."

I smile and start walking him to the door. "We wouldn't want you getting your ass kicked, so I guess you're free to go."

He opens the door and starts backing out. "You have my number."

I nod. "I do."

Turning around, he walks away, causing my head to go crazy with thoughts the second I'm left alone.

Holy shit . . . I just had sex with two guys within two days; two insanely, sexy guys that I could only dream of even kissing.

I take in a deep breath and plop down on the couch. That's

when I notice a missed text on my phone. I grab my phone off the coffee table and see Kyan's name across the screen.

My heart speeds up.

Kyan: I want to see you tomorrow night. Meet me at my place at seven.

I grip onto my phone and type back with shaky fingers. Looks like I'll be telling Kyan about my little date night with Hunter tomorrow. I know he said this is what he wants, but I still feel weird about all this.

Me: Should I dress comfortably? Is this a training session?

He replies a couple minutes later.

Kyan: You can wear anything you want. I'm here to please you, Calla. I'll see you then.

My heart skips a beat as I read his message for a third time. I have no idea how to respond to that . . . so I don't.

I don't know if I can survive these boys . . .

Chapter Eleven

Kyan

I'M IN MY OFFICE FINISHING up paperwork when Erica appears in my doorway and lightly knocks on the opened door.

I tilt my head and look up. "What's up, Erica?"

She points behind her. "There's a guy here asking for you? He says he really needs to see you. Says he's an old friend. He seems a little out of it or drunk or something."

Shit . . .

I let out a frustrated breath and grip the top of my desk. "Send him in. I'll take care of him."

A few seconds later Bryant walks in dressed in a wrinkled suit and looking as if he hasn't slept in days. His tired, brown eyes land on mine as he closes the door behind us.

Fighting to keep my shit in check, I nod to the chair in front of my desk. "Take a seat." I clench my jaw and swallow in anger as I watch him sitting there looking back at me. Doesn't he realize how hard it is for me not to kill him? "What do you want?"

He leans forward and runs his hands over his face before looking back up. His blonde, curly hair is long and out of control, and his face looks as if he hasn't shaven in weeks. "I can't fucking sleep, man." He rubs his hands together. "She's killing me and I don't know what the hell to do."

Okay, now I'm convinced he's lost his fucking mind. He wants to sit in my fucking chair and talk about the woman he fucked me over with.

Do not kill this sad fucker, Kyan . . .

I stand up, lean over the desk and slam my fists down, causing him to jump back. My hands grip onto the desk and I can feel my veins popping from my neck. I'm beyond ready to rip his throat out. "What the fuck, Bryant!" I tilt my head up and lock my eyes with his. "Jessica is not my problem. Your relationship with her is not my problem. In fact, I want nothing to do with either of you."

He stands up from his seat and swipes an arm over my desk, knocking the papers off. "You're the one that decided to let a fucking woman come between ten years of friendship. Ten years, bro. Now I can't even get you to answer a simple text, and I have to sit at home and listen to my woman compare me to you; how you did this and you did that. Do you think that's easy for me? Huh? Knowing that she's with me but wants you?"

I lean my head back and let out a forced breath. It's going to take a lot of strength to not jump over this desk and kick the shit out of him. "No," I growl out. "That's where you're wrong. *You* let a woman get in the way of our friendship. You broke the code, bro. She wasn't just a random hook up. She was the girl I was going to fucking marry. I don't give a shit what she wants now, and I definitely don't give a shit about what you want. You both should have thought about the fucking future when you were both fucking me in the ass. That's all I can do now, and *my* future sure as fuck doesn't involve the two of you."

I stand up straight and flex my jaw as he stares at me. "You know what? Get. The. Fuck. Out. The two of you deserve misery together, and when you get home tell Jessica to fuck herself and forget about me. I've already forgotten about her."

Bryant's nostrils flare as he just stands there, looking straight ahead. I've held this anger in for far too fucking long. Seeing the look in his eyes tells me that he's definitely feeling my hatred and betrayal. Good.

He nods his head a few times before shaking it and turning to face the door. "Take it easy, *old friend.*"

As soon as the door closes I grab my desk and flip it over, before grabbing the chair he was just sitting in and breaking it against the wall. My blood is pumping so damn fast that I'm seeing red. I don't need this shit right now. I don't need to think, or feel.

"Fuck you!" I kick my desk. "That fucking asshole."

My door opens, and without looking up I scream. "Get the fuck out!"

Whoever it was decides not to question my outburst. The door quickly closes and I'm left standing here, coming undone.

Leaving my office a mess, I grab my jacket and lock the door behind me. I look straight ahead, jaw tense as I walk for the door. I feel eyes on me, but right now I don't care. I just need to get away from all this bullshit. I need fucking freedom.

Rushing outside, I quickly straddle my Harley and head home so I can change out of these damn sweats.

I'M ON THE ELEVATOR, STARING at the numbers like an idiot. My finger is hovering over the button labeled with a six, and I want to press it so fucking bad right now that I'm about to say fuck everything. It's a little after six and Calla is supposed to be at my door in an hour. I know I won't be home by then and there's no way I'm blowing her off.

"Shit." I push the number six and wait for the elevator door to open again. Without overthinking it, I walk down the hall and stop in front of door number 629 before I can change my mind. I might be stupid for doing this, but at the moment I just don't give a fuck.

I knock and grip the doorframe, waiting for Calla to answer. I know she's here because I saw her white Jeep downstairs. I parked my bike right next to it.

A few seconds later I hear her friend yelling for her to get the door, and then the door opens to Calla curiously looking me up and down. She's standing there with the cutest *surprised* expression I have ever seen. She pulls her pouty bottom lip into her mouth before releasing it.

"Kyan . . ." Her curious eyes meet mine and I instantly see a change in her expression. "Is everything alright?"

She looks a little worried as she waits for my response. The truth is . . . I really don't know how to answer that without lying.

"No." I swallow hard and look down at her while gripping the doorframe tighter. "I need some air. Come with me?"

She glances over her shoulder at her roommate and some guy that are sitting on the couch arguing over some movie, before turning back to face me. "Yeah . . . ok, sure." She reaches for her jacket, pulls it off the coatrack, and slips into it. "I'll be back later, Tori. I'm going with Kyan."

"I want all the details . . ."

Calla quickly slams the door behind her before giving me an awkward smile. "She's on drugs. Don't mind her." She clears her throat and walks past me. "I could really use some air as well. Those two have been driving me crazy for the last two hours."

I place my hand on the small of her back and guide her toward the elevator. Just the feel of her back is enough to make me want to put my hands in other places.

She smiles up at me as the elevator opens for us. "Where are we going?"

I wait until after Calla steps into the elevator, before stepping in myself and hitting the 1st floor. "Just somewhere I like to go when I need to breathe and forget about everything."

I offer her no more information as we make our way out of the elevator and into the cool, night air.

She stops walking and gives me a nervous look when I stop in front of my motorcycle. "Whoa. Motorcycles sort of scare the shit out of me. I love to watch others ride, but . . ."

I grab onto her hip and give her a reassuring smile. "I would let myself get hurt before I ever put you in danger. Trust me."

She thinks on that for a second before nodding and allowing me to place my helmet on her head. I stand here for a second and take in her beauty as she stands there in a pair of skintight jeans, black boots, and a little black jacket. Her hair is pulled to the side, sticking out from under my helmet, and it honestly makes me smile just from looking at her. She's waiting on me, looking up at me as if she's putting all her trust in me. It makes me feel at ease. I like it.

Straddling my bike, I reach out my hand and help her onto the back. "Wrap your arms around my waist." She reaches around me and wraps her arms around me so tightly that I almost can't breathe. "Whoa. It's okay." I rub my hand over hers to calm her nerves a little. "I won't go fast until you tell me it's okay. You can trust me."

She leans her head against my back and loosens her grip on me. "Really? My ex took me for a ride on his friend's bike once and that asshole definitely tricked me by telling me he'd drive slow. He didn't."

I feel a small ache in my chest from the tone in her voice. She sounds pained. I don't like hearing her that way. "Really," I reply. "I would never do that to you. Trust is a big issue for me. If I give you a reason not to trust me, then how can I expect you to not do the same?"

"I like that," she says, locking her hands together. "I'm ready now."

I take off slow, wanting her to see that I'm true to my word. Making a woman feel as if I would ever hurt her and give her reason not to trust me doesn't sit well with me. A woman should feel safe and cared for by a man. The problem is . . . some women just don't want that. I learned the hard way.

We ride for a while, the two of us just enjoying the sights and the cool air, until I finally pull up at my favorite spot. It's not much really, just a big open field with a few trees, but it's always given me a feeling of freedom and peace.

Killing the engine, I help her off my bike before pulling the helmet from her head and setting it down.

I take off walking into the middle of nowhere and I hear her following behind me. I usually come here alone, but having her with me sort of feels nice. I have a feeling that she has been hurt in the past and maybe she needs this place just as much as I do.

Once we get far enough into the middle of nowhere, I stop and take off my jacket, tossing it down beside me.

Calla stops right next to me and just watches in silence as I strip my shirt off next and roll it up before laying it on my jacket.

"Come here." I grab her hand and guide her down to the ground so that she's lying on my jacket, using my shirt as a pillow.

I drop down beside her and lay with my hands interlocked behind my head. When I glance beside me, she's staring up at the night sky and picking at the grass beside her.

"It's nice out here," she says softly. "So peaceful and beautiful."

Looking at her here beside me, looking so at ease and peaceful, I realize she's never looked so damn beautiful. "Definitely beautiful," I admit.

I close my eyes and try to force all the bad memories out of my head. Seeing Bryant today brought up a bunch of old emotions that I thought I had control over. Losing it like I did only proved that I was wrong; so damn wrong.

"Do you come here a lot?" I hear her shift beside me so I turn to look at her. She's lying on her side with her hand propped below her head as her eyes look at me with sincerity. "I can see why this place helps you clear your head."

Sitting up, I run my hands through my hair. "Yeah. I've been coming here for a few years now. Usually when I come here, I'm alone." I relax into her touch when I feel her hand rub over my back. "I've been controlling myself better lately, so I haven't had to come as much, but today I had an unwanted visitor, so . . . here I am."

I hear her moving beside me, and after a few seconds, she's on her knees behind me, rubbing my shoulders. "Relax, Kyan." She leans close to my neck as she rubs her thumbs in circles between my shoulder blades. "You're really tense."

I find myself moaning and leaning further into her touch. Her hands feel so damn good. "That feels amazing."

She lets out a tiny laugh. "Thanks." She's silent for a second before speaking again. "I spent many years rubbing my little sister to sleep when we were younger, so . . . I guess there's *one* thing I should thank her for."

Reaching up, I grab her arm and kiss it, before pulling her around in front of me. Grabbing the back of her neck, I lay her down in the grass and spread her legs with my knee. "It's really hard feeling your hands on me without me wanting to touch you back. Do you realize that?"

Her eyes look down at my chest and I catch her cheeks turn slightly pink. It's not the easiest seeing her in the dark, but I can see enough to know that she wants me to touch her just as much as I want to.

She locks her eyes with mine before shaking her head and hiding her face behind her hand. "Kyan . . . I was with a guy last night. I don't usually do this."

I feel a small ache in my chest until I remember that is what I told her to do. This is what I wanted for both of us. I just never expected it to be my brother. I grab her chin and rub my thumb over her soft lips. "You talked to him about us?" She swallows and nods her head. "Then there's nothing to be ashamed of. We both know about each other so you're not doing anything wrong. I want *you* to be pleased. That's all I can offer."

A part of me almost feels glad that Hunter has already talked to her about us. The last thing I want to do is make her feel awkward with the fact that we're brothers.

This is the first time that I have ever been with the same woman as my brother. This is the last thing I thought I'd be doing, but I can't stop, and I have no claim over Calla so I have no right to ask him to back off.

The weird part is . . . knowing that she's been with another man, any man, only makes me want to please her better than her last. I may be selfish for this, but I want to be her best.

"Do you want me inside you, Calla?" I pull her leg up and run my hand up her thigh. "We can stop what we're doing right now . . . if that's what you want."

I run my other hand over her neck and feel her swallow under my touch. "I always seem to want you inside me," she admits. "Even at the most inappropriate times."

Her words cause me to lose control, and before I know it I have her standing up and I'm on my knees, undressing her while running my lips over every inch of her exposed flesh.

Once I have her completely naked, I run my hands down her back, stopping on her ass. I look up at her before swirling my tongue around her clit and sucking it into my mouth.

She lets out a small moan and grips onto my hair for encouragement. This only drives me more. I want to taste her in the best way possible and do something that I know she'll enjoy.

With my mouth still on her pussy, I wrap one of her legs around my shoulder before doing the other, holding onto her back for support while standing to my feet.

She lets out a nervous squeal while giving my hair the death grip. I would never drop her, but I think it's cute that she's scared. I'm sure no other man has ever done this for her and it gives me the drive I need to make her feel *everything* her body needs.

I slide my tongue between her folds, tasting her as if she's never been licked before. That thought makes me work my tongue in ways I didn't even know was possible.

Slightly arching her back, she moans out in pleasure as I suck her clit hard and without mercy. I can tell that she loves it, because her thighs are squeezing my face so hard that it hurts. I dig my face deeper into her pussy and allow her to squeeze me.

"Kyan!" She pulls my hair as I release her clit and work my tongue over every last sensitive spot. "Keep going. Oh God . . . right there."

She leans her body over my head while scratching her

nails down my back. That's when I feel her come undone in my mouth, leaving her release on my tongue. Her whole body is trembling and I'm standing here holding her as tight as I can to be sure she can enjoy this moment with the trust that I'll hold her up.

"Kyan . . ." She's out of breath as she repeats my name over and over. "Holy shit, Kyan. What do you do to me?"

"Please you," I respond. "Show you that you're worth every last bit of pleasure I can give you."

Gripping her waist, I slide her off my shoulders and wrap both of my hands into her hair as she stands there trying to catch her breath. Then, I slowly lower her to the ground so that she's on her knees, kissing her until she's lying flat on her back.

Pulling away from our kiss, I grab my jacket and quickly dig into my pocket for the condom before stripping myself of my jeans.

Calla sits back up and eagerly licks her lips while reaching for the top of my boxers. I love seeing how desperate she looks to have them off of me.

"Pull my boxers down to where you want them," I say with a smirk, remembering our photo shoot.

She playfully looks up at me while jerking my boxers down my legs and forcing me to step out of them. Wasting no time, she softly trails her fingertips along the backs of my legs before stopping at my waist. I lift an eyebrow and watch her as she runs her hand down my stomach, before wrapping both of her hands around my cock.

"Is it weird that I find your dick to be beautiful?" She whispers as if she's unsure that she wants me to hear. "I've never really had the urge to do this before."

Before I can say anything, her lips are around my cock and her tongue is swirling around the head. I moan at the feel of her sweet tongue tasting me. She's got the most beautiful fucking mouth I've ever seen and it's wrapped around my cock right now.

It takes her a few seconds to get used to my size, but then she's pleasuring me as if she wants nothing more than to return the orgasm I just gave her.

My hand is wrapped into the back of her thick hair and I dig my teeth into my lip as she moves faster and harder. It feels so damn good that I'm about to lose it and come in her mouth. I don't want that. I want to come inside her pussy.

Tugging back on her hair, I pull her away until my cock springs free from the grasp of her lips. I drop down to my knees and kiss her so hard that I have to hold the back of her head to avoid it hitting the ground. I run my tongue over her lips before sucking her bottom lip into my mouth, causing her to moan against my lips.

"I was about to come," I say out of breath. "I want to be inside you when I do."

I quickly flip her over and lay her flat on her stomach, before running my tongue up the middle of her back while ripping the condom open. Admiring her body, I roll the condom on, before slipping an arm around her waist to slightly raise her body.

I can feel her body jerk each time that my cock brushes against her entrance, and this makes me want to fuck her so hard that she won't be able to sit on my bike when we leave. I need to control myself.

Leaning over her body, I suck on her neck while trusting my cock into the tightness of her pussy. She cries out and grips the grass.

"Does my cock feel good in your tight little pussy, Calla?" I grip her hair and move my hips in a circular motion. "Do you want me to fuck you hard or gentle?" I slowly pull out before gently thrusting back into her." She moans out. "You like it slow and gentle so that you can feel every single inch?"

"Yes, Kyan. I want to feel you inside me," she whimpers. "Every. Single. Inch."

Wrapping an arm around her neck, I pull her toward me and run my lip under her ear. "Then I'll give it to you nice and slow. Every. Single. Inch of it."

I begin thrusting my hips slow and deep, causing her to moan out with each thrust, only causing me to go deeper and slower.

I usually like it fast and hard, but there's no denying the way her body is making me feel at the moment. The sensation is almost unreal, and I find myself wanting to bust my load in her right now.

"I want you to come with me, Calla." I kiss her neck. "Tell me when you're about to come."

Reaching below her, I rub her clit while fucking her nice and slow. After a few minutes I feel her start to tremble in my arms.

"Now, Kyan." She grips onto the grass as her pussy clench-es around me, bringing me to orgasm at the same time. I push in as deep as I can, and allow my cum to fill the condom.

"Fuck, Calla." I kiss the back of her neck before grabbing her face and pulling it back enough so that I can run my tongue over her lips before kissing her roughly. "I don't think I can ever get enough of being inside you."

Falling over in the grass, I pull her onto me so that she's lying on my chest. We both just lay here, breathing heavily and holding each other while staring up at the night sky.

I swear I never want to move from this spot. Everything about this moment just feels so fucking peaceful. I'm laying here naked, under the night sky with the most beautiful woman on earth. It all seems perfect.

If only it were that easy . . .

Chapter Twelve

Calla

BITING MY LIP, I STARE down at the fancy, silver envelope sitting in front of me. I've been staring at it off and on for the last hour, trying to decide if I want to open it.

When Tori and I got done with the *Anderson Wedding,* I made a quick stop by the mailbox to grab the mail on the way back up. Everything was bills and junk mail, everything except this . . . this stupid, fancy envelope.

I read my sister's name for the twentieth time, feeling as if I'm caught in some kind of stupid nightmare. "Chrissy Reynolds . . ." I can't believe I'm looking at this right now. It's been two years since we have spoken. Two whole years and now here I am, sitting in front of her envelope, looking at it as if it's going to bite me. The bad thing is, it probably will.

"Open it, Calla." Tori looks at me from her spot on the couch. "It's just going to torture you if you don't. Why put it off longer and let that whore bag win?"

I nervously play with the end of my ponytail while staring angrily at the envelope. "Look at the envelope, Tori." I pick it up and slam it back down onto the table. "It's a wedding invitation. I don't need to open it to see that. She's already won and she knows it. The whole world knows it."

Tori tugs me back down to the couch and hands me the envelope. "No. . . . What the whole world knows is that she's a twofaced, conniving bitch that deserves to get her expensive heels shoved up her high maintenance ass. No one likes the bitch." She bumps her shoulder against mine and we both laugh at the truth in her words. "Now open the envelope before I rip it up and toss it out the window. Then, I'll personally drive to Wisconsin, take her fancy stiletto off her foot, and shove it where nothing else has ever been. Damn prude. "

I turn my head away and take a long, deep breath while opening the envelope with shaky hands. "I hate this." I pull the black and silver paper out and hold my breath as my whole world officially breaks apart and crumbles in front of me. I feel like I've just been stabbed in the heart by one of my sister's *expensive* heels.

My eyes stay glued to the pretty lettering as the wetness begins to slide down my cheeks, wetting the fancy paper. I feel like I'm in some kind of daze as I sit here staring at the invitation.

"Fuck it, Calla," Tori says in an attempt to soothe me as I stare like a fucking zombie. I feel her hand on my back as she looks over my shoulder. "She's not worth your tears. Dry your face off." She dramatically wipes her arms over my face, causing me to laugh through my tears.

Nodding my head, I drop the invitation down onto the table and grab the envelope from my lap. I get ready to rip it up until I notice that there's a small piece of paper stuffed inside.

Tori notices it at the same time I do and quickly grabs the envelope away, saving it from my destruction. "You don't need to read this right now, honey. One thing at a time, but don't rip it up. See what the bitch has to say first." She reaches out and wipes away another stray tear. "You're better than this, better than her, and better than them. You're better than anyone that I know. *Never* forget that."

I nod my head and close my eyes. I hate feeling this way. I don't know why I let her affect me this way after two years. Maybe it's the fact that she actually has the nerve to invite me to her fucking wedding. I don't know what would ever make her think that I would actually want to be there for that. I can't tell if I'm more angry or shocked. I'm definitely both. I feel like someone has reached into my chest and is twisting my heart.

Tori stands up and reaches for her purse, looking pissed at the world. "Enough of this bullshit. You need to get out. We're going to go out, grab a few drinks, and have fun. No thinking. No caring. No crying. Call up Kyan and I'll call up Brad and we'll make a night of it."

Kyan . . . My heart swells at the memories of last night. The sex was great, don't get me wrong, but the best part was just lying in his arms afterwards without a single care in the world. What I wouldn't give right now to go back to that moment and forget this day all together. We laid there for what seemed like hours, talking and enjoying the freedom. He asked me about my job and my family, my interests and anything that I would expect a boyfriend to want to know. Whenever I said something funny, I found comfort in the vibration of his chest as he let loose and just lived in the moment with me. Oddly, I crave for that feeling right now.

"I can't just call Kyan up and ask him to go on a double date, Tori. It's not like that with us. He's got two businesses to run and he's not my boyfriend. He's just . . . he's . . ." I stop and let out a frustrated breath. "He's busy."

Thinking about Kyan only seems to make my head hurt at the moment. I want nothing more than to ask him to hang out with me, but I'm afraid he'll say no and remind me of the fact that we can never be anything more. The thought causes my chest to ache and I fill up with anxiety.

"He might not be."

"Huh?" I look up from my phone that I didn't even realize I was now holding.

Tori grins and points to my phone. "Send him a text. It's not going to hurt to ask. Then go to your room and change out of that work attire crap and throw on something cute and flirty."

I watch Tori as she rushes to her room and flicks on the light. I can stand here and drown in my self-pity all night *or* I can just say screw it, ask Kyan to come out with us, and forget all about my sister and her stupid invitation.

"Screw this," I mutter while pulling up Kyan's number and sending him a text. I drop my phone down onto the table and hurry to my room to change.

After throwing on a black and silver tunic and a pair of gray leggings, I slip into what I call my *rock girl* boots and pull my hair into a sloppy bun above my right shoulder.

I feel a nervous knot form in my stomach as I walk back into the living room and reach for my phone. My heart jumps when I see two text messages from Kyan. Taking a deep breath, I pull up the messages and read them.

> *Kyan: I can leave work now and meet you.*

> *Kyan: Where are we going? I'm grabbing my things and walking out the door now.*

Oh my God . . .

My heart does this stupid little dance as I quickly text him back. I feel as if my fingers can't move fast enough and I find myself mentally yelling at my fingers to work.

> *Me: You really didn't have to leave work for me, only if*

you're free. No pressure. We'll be at Bare.

My phone vibrates immediately with his response.

Kyan: Oh, I'd definitely rather be spending time with you instead of in this stupid office. See you soon.

I'm ashamed that Tori walks out and catches me with this stupid, silly grin on my face. I know I look ridiculously happy, because she's got her head tilted and she's clapping happily like a two year old.

"Looks like Kyan wasn't busy after all. Imagine that." She looks me over, checking out my *going out* attire before nodding in approval and whistling. "Now that looks hot. This is the Calla that I like to see. The fun one that isn't always worrying about everyone else and what they think." She glances down at my boots. "I seriously might have to borrow that outfit sometime." She throws her hands on her hips and smirks while pushing out her breasts. "You likie?"

She's wearing a pair of black skinny jeans and a white off-the-shoulder shirt that says: *Objects in shirt are bigger than they appear.*

I laugh as I reach for my purse. "Yup. That shirt is totally you." I shove my phone into my purse and loop my arm through hers. "Looks like we're going to *Club Bare*. Kyan is leaving work to meet us there."

She turns to me and lifts her eyebrows. "Leaving work, huh? Yeah, someone just wants to be fuck buddies my ass."

I push her with my hip. "We're *just* having fun. I'm sure he was about to leave work anyways. Now shut up and let's go before I change my mind."

CLUB BARE IS PACKED WHEN we arrive, but we somehow manage to snag up a table and cover it with all of our crap. The only way to keep a table in a place like this it to make it as blatantly clear as possible that it's taken. I guess the same could go for your woman as well. The only way to keep her in a place like this is to make it clear that she's with you.

That is exactly what Brad is doing right now. Tori is standing in front of the table and Brad is so far up her ass that I almost believe he's literally up there.

"What do you want to drink? You can stay here and watch our table while Brad and I go get the drinks." Tori is reaching in her purse for her wallet when Kyan's voice sounds next to my ear.

"Am I first to claim you tonight?" I feel his lips brush my ear as he smiles against it. "I had to be sure to beat all the other assholes to you."

I nod my head and laugh as I turn my head to look up at him. "You're definitely first, Mr. Wilder. Lucky you, I guess."

He steps around the table and I about die on the spot when my eyes land on what he's wearing. I notice Tori clearly checking him out too, as if Brad doesn't even exist at the moment.

His thick legs are being hugged by a pair of form fitting, black trousers and his broad chest is covered in a white dress shirt, rolled up to the elbows, with a black vest. His tie hangs loosely around his neck and his hair looks as if he's just finished having the best fuck of his life. In other words, he looks *dangerously irresistible.* I can guarantee that every female mouth dropped on his way over to this table and they're busy wiping the drool from their damn chins right now.

He smiles at Tori and says hello before introducing himself to Brad. He leans into Brad's shoulder with all the confidence in the world and says something before turning back to us. "So what will it be, ladies?"

Tori raises a brow and twists her face up in thought before settling on a beer, as well as the rest of us, and before we know it Kyan has one of the waitresses over taking our orders and smiling at Kyan as if she's the happiest girl in the world.

Back up, hussy . . .

Tori smiles at Kyan and her eyes follow him all the way to his seat. "So . . ." She pulls out her own chair and takes a seat, as so does Brad. "Were you done working for the day?"

Kyan thanks the waitress and grabs for one of the beers, while loosening his tie some more. "Nah. I'm never really done with work."

"I see." Tori grins at me like an idiot, so I quickly kick her leg and change the subject.

We spend the first hour or so just hanging out at our table, drinking and talking, and I have to admit that Chrissy's invitation is the last thing on my mind tonight. That invitation can kiss my ass. Time is flying by and everyone is getting along as if we've done this a hundred times before. It's comfortable. I haven't had this kind of fun out with friends in what seems like forever.

It seems that a lot of people here know who Kyan is and treats him with so much respect that I can't help but to smile as I watch him interact with others that randomly stop by to say hi. He's so different than most men. He doesn't have to *try*. People just naturally like and respect him and he doesn't seem to let that go to his head. It makes me happy to just be around him.

"Alright," Tori says while grabbing Brad's hand. "This is a lot of fun and all, but I need to move. I'm too young to just sit here." She giggles as Brad pulls her into his arms and bites her neck. "We'll be out on the dance floor. You two don't have too much fun."

Kyan tilts his head at me and grins before taking a swig of his beer and setting it back down. "Come on." He grabs my hand and starts pulling me out into the crowd. Luckily I'm on my third beer, so I'm feeling a bit loose and am starting to not worry about all the sets of eyes that seem to keep following us around.

Kyan pretends to not notice all the girls gawking at him, but it has definitely caught my attention.

"You dance?" I question as he slips an arm around my waist and pulls me against him.

He slowly grinds his hips to the music in such a seductive way that a breath escapes me. I seriously had no idea that he could move his body like that.

He leans into my ear and laughs against it. "Surprised? Don't let the suit fool you." Moving behind me, he runs his hand up my arm and pulls it around his neck, while grinding his hips against my ass. I feel his lips against my ear again. "It's been a while, but I *never* forget how to move my body."

Oh God . . .

I feel my body moving in rhythm with his as if we've done this a million times before. One of his arms is around my neck and the other around my waist as we move to the slow beat, his body controlling mine. It feels too much like the bedroom and I instantly feel the heat rush through my body at the memories.

His hand runs up my neck until my head is tilted back and his lips are running across my face. They trace my hairline, nose, and cheeks, but never stop on my lips. Still, just the feel of his breath so close to mine gets my heart racing.

We dance for a while until he notices that I'm out of breath. Obviously I'm not in as good of shape as him and I started to break a sweat at least twenty minutes ago.

"Sorry," I say while fighting to catch my breath. "I don't

dance much."

He runs his hand under my hair, along the back of my neck and smiles. "Don't be." Lacing his fingers through mine, he pulls me through the crowd and over to stand next to the bar. He leans in so I can hear him. "I haven't done this in a while, but being here with you makes me forget about all the fucked up stress of work. I finally remember what it's like to relax and enjoy myself."

He picks my chin up and runs his thumb over my bottom lip. "I'm happy you invited me out tonight. I desperately needed this."

I find myself smiling against his thumb. "Well I'm glad you came." I lean beside him against the bar. "I didn't think you'd come. I figured you'd be too busy working."

He waves over a bartender and orders us a couple beers. I seriously have no idea where Tori and Brad are, and for once I could care less. Usually when I go out with Tori I hate when I can't find her, even when I am with someone else. Right now . . . I'm perfectly fine just having Kyan close by.

Tossing down some cash, he grabs both beer bottles in his right hand before grabbing my hand with his free one.

I see him glance back at me and smile when he notices an open pool table. Pulling me behind him, he grabs up an empty table and sets our drinks down.

"You down for another game?" He raises a brow. "Maybe this time I won't have to carry you home?"

I push his chest a few times and laugh at my stupid behavior that first night. I was hoping the end of that night was just some kind of weird dream.

"I'm down." I watch him as he watches me. "What?"

He shakes his head. "Nothing."

"Nothing?" I step closer to him and grab his tie, bringing

my lips close to his. He looks down at my lips before bringing his eyes up to meet mine. The pained look in them has me clearing my throat and releasing his tie. I grab for my cue stick and smile as if that moment never happened. The last thing I want to do is make him feel uncomfortable.

"You break this time." I stand back and cross my arms. "I'm pretty sure since I'm sober this time that I'll be kicking your ass." I lean over the table and grin at him as he concentrates on breaking. "I promise not to tell too many people."

He looks up at me and keeps his eyes there while breaking. I'm surprised to see how good of a shot he still made. It was a nice, solid hit.

"Show off," I mutter.

I stand back and watch as he continuously hits solid after solid into the pockets until he's down to just one ball. Then, he misses on purpose.

"Really!" I shriek. I slap the end of the pool table and grab for my beer. "You tricked me our first night. You didn't play nearly that good."

He gives me a sexy grin as I set my beer down and prepare for my shot. "I didn't want to scare you away and blow my chances of another game with you."

"Liar," I say.

"I'm dead serious." He leans over me and runs his lips up my neck just as I'm about to take a shot. My hand loses grip and I hear him laugh in my ear. "Oops."

I playfully elbow him in the stomach, causing him to back up an inch. "That's cheating. Now back off, big guy. I'm not giving up so easily."

We both laugh and I can't stop looking at him. He's so damn beautiful. That smile . . . how did I miss that it's the most beautiful smile in the world? I could seriously just stand here all night and watch his mouth and not have a single care in the world. That definitely gives me a reason as to why I should have a care in the world.

No attachments . . . Just for fun.

I have to keep repeating this to myself through the rest of the game. I lost count of how many times I had to mentally voice it to myself.

Tori and Brad appear toward the end of the second game, watching as Kyan takes his shot. Tori takes one look at the pool table before giving me a look hinting that I'm pathetic. Maybe I needed a few more beers to play better. I swear I was better last time, but I'm wrong. Kyan was playing me and it worked. He's a pro at everything he does. It makes me want to bite him.

I raise my stick to Tori as she's about to open her mouth. "Don't even say it."

She shrugs her shoulders. "I wasn't going to say anything about how badly you're losing." She shrugs again. "Really."

Kyan wins yet another game, so I set my cue stick down and poke him in the ribs. "You're lucky you're so damn cute. I usually don't take losing so lightly."

He grabs me by the waist and picks me up off the ground, kissing the top of my head, before setting me back down. "I'm going to pay the tab so we can get going." He grabs the empty beer bottles and walks through the crowd.

"Holy fuck!" Tori grabs onto my arm and pulls me to her. "He is really something else; so, so, so much better than Jordan. He's almost unreal. Is he real?" She turns to Brad. "Sorry." Then she turns back to me. "But damn!"

Brad just shrugs his shoulders and says, "It's all good," and finishes off his drink. "I'll be right back."

Brushing strands of his golden hair out of his face, Brad kisses Tori on the mouth before walking away and toward the bar.

"Can I trade him in?" She raises both brows. "I'll give you one week with Brad if I can have Kyan for one night. Just one night and I bet he'll make up for a year's worth of sex with Brad."

I push her and cover my mouth in surprise. "That is so mean to say."

We both look over at the bar. Kyan is standing there with confidence, knowing that one of the girls will fight to get to him as soon as they are free, while Brad keeps jumping around and waving his arms, looking like a helpless little boy.

"He's not that bad." I lie. "I mean . . . he's cute. He has that going for him. He's just like a little puppy. Girls love puppies."

She rolls her eyes and pulls out some gloss, coating her plump lips. "Not me, Calla. Definitely not me."

"Then why are you with him?"

She gives me a confused look and shakes her head to herself. "I don't know. I guess to keep busy. It helps sometimes to have sex with someone that you know you won't fall for. It saves you from getting hurt. I guess Brad is safe . . . I know I won't get too attached, and so I keep holding on. Men scare me. Real men that is."

I stand here in a daze and let her words really sink in. Kyan is exactly the opposite. He's the guy that I see myself falling for, except I can't make myself stop having sex with him. My body physically aches for his touch whenever he's near. I don't want to stop, no matter what the consequences are.

I feel a hand on my arm so I turn beside me. Some dark haired guy, wearing a polo shirt and a pair of khakis, smiles at me.

"You're too beautiful to be standing here alone." He holds up his beer. "Can I get you a drink?"

I shake my head and offer him a friendly smile. "I'm not here alone." I lean into him so he can hear me over the music. "Thank you, but no."

When I look over his shoulder, Kyan is walking with his hand on Brad's shoulder. I see Brad thanking him, so I'm guessing he took care of his tab to save him the trouble from bouncing around.

His eyes look away from Brad to meet mine, and his jaw steels. I can clearly see his hard body tense up.

"Are you sure?" The guy places his hand on my arm and leans into my ear. "I don't see you with anyone. Just one drink."

Kyan's hand grips the guy's shoulder, pulling him out of my face. "She's here with someone." Pretending that the guy doesn't even exist, Kyan smiles at me and grabs the back of my neck. "Let me give you a ride back home."

Mumbling something under his breath, the guy turns and walks away, clearly realizing that he has no chance against Kyan.

"Okay," I say with a smile. "I guess you sort of owe me a ride home after kicking my ass in pool so many times. It's the least you can do."

Tori gives me a huge, face-ripping smile and hands her keys to Brad. "I'm going to have Brad drive me home and we'll pick up my car tomorrow morning. I'll see you at home."

Kyan says bye to Tori and Brad, before pulling me through the crowd, keeping his eyes on me instead of all the girls that seem to be staring at him in passing.

Why do I want to choke all of these girls? Every damn one of them is making it so obvious that it seriously looks desperate. The good thing is that it doesn't even seem to faze Kyan like it would most men.

We have small talk the entire way back to the apartment and I find myself cracking silly jokes all the way into the building. I'm ashamed to say this always happens when I get too tired. Mix it with alcohol and it's worse than you can imagine. Sometimes I want to run from myself. It's that bad.

Kyan holds the elevator, letting me step in first.

"I hope you don't have to work in the morning." He leans against the wall and smiles when I do. "I'd hate to see how that shoot comes out."

I slap his arm and laugh. "No, I don't, thank goodness, but I can guarantee I would still rock that wedding," I say, pointing at him.

He smiles at me and places his arm on the small of my back as the elevator stops on the sixth floor. "I believe it," he says. "You're amazing at what you do. I could see that from the shoot we did. It comes naturally for you."

I find myself smiling bigger than I probably should be by his comment. "Thanks. That means a lot."

Pulling out my key, I unlock the door and turn back to him. He steps closer, bringing our bodies together. His eyes meet mine as he brings his lips down and kisses the side of my mouth.

His lips linger there for a second, causing my heart to pound with anticipation. I want his lips to crush mine, but they don't.

He pulls away, grinding his jaw as he looks into my eyes. "Goodnight, Calla."

I swallow as I look up at him. "Goodnight, Kyan." I grab his tie and tug on it. "Thanks for tonight. It was a lot of fun. I needed it really bad."

He nods once while looking me up and down. "I forgot to tell you that you look incredibly sexy tonight. It's taking a lot for me to just walk away instead of inviting myself in."

My heart races as my eyes lock with his.

Does he want me to invite him in? Do I ask him? Crap!

He's the first to break the silence. "We need to catch up on some training. Meet me at the gym around noon?" He rubs his thumb over my bottom lip. "Can you manage that?"

I nod my head and open the door behind me. "See you then." I smile. " I think I can manage."

The elevator opens up to Tori, so Kyan flashes me a smile and quickly catches the door as Tori steps out and tiredly stumbles to the door.

She walks past me and tosses her purse down onto the ground. "I'm so hungry. Make me food," she whines.

I pull my eyes away from Kyan and walk into the apartment, shutting the door behind me.

Now that I'm back here and alone . . . well with Tori, I feel that ache in my chest again as I remember the invitation.

Tonight's going to be a long night . . .

Chapter Thirteen

Calla

I MET KYAN AT THE gym this afternoon, spent about an hour training with him, and then went to the mall with Tori. Now here I am, lying down on the couch, and relaxing with one of the sexiest men alive: Ryan Guzman.

He looks so incredibly sexy when he's moving his body that it reminds me of Kyan at the club last night. That thought keeps me smiling. I could lay here all day and watch him, forgetting about everything else, so that is my plan.

Tori is curled up in the chair with her Funyuns, watching the movie just as hard as I am. This is about the only way I can get her to shut up: a sexy guy on TV and her favorite snack.

My whole body is sore from my workout this afternoon, so every time I move trying to get comfortable, I let out a slight groan.

"Shut your face over there," Tori complains.

"Really though . . ." I toss a pillow at her face. "You're over there chomping on those Funyuns as if your life depends on it. Close your mouth when you chew, asshole."

Shh . . ." She growls at me and turns up the volume. "You've been moaning and groaning since we were at the mall. Tell Kyan not to fuck you so hard next time, because it's really ruining my day."

I sit up and roll my eyes. "He didn't. I had a personal training session with him. The gym was full of people this time. Nothing happened."

Her ears perk up, and suddenly her attention is on me. "This time?"

Crap . . . my stupid, big mouth.

She hits the pause button and sits up straight, suddenly interested in listening to me speak, when before all she was interested in was having me shut the hell up. "Have you and Kyan had sex at the gym? If you did then I really need to know because that is fucking *hot* and exciting.

"Maybe . . ." I lift a brow. "Is someone suddenly curious about the gym, because a few seconds ago I remember you telling me to shut my face."

"Maybe . . . and that was before sex at the gym crossed my mind." She grins, encouraging me to go on. "So did you?"

"I shouldn't even tell you, but yes, and it *was* hot and exciting. That's all you need to know." I reach for my phone and start scrolling through my emails, trying to get away from this conversation. "It was later at night so no one was there. That's all you're getting."

"I so hate you." She tosses the pillow back at me. "At least tell me where at in the gym? You can't just tell me Kyan fucked your brains out at the gym and leave it at that."

My eyes widen when I notice a reply email from Olivia Powers. "The shower . . ." I trail off while quickly opening her email to see an attachment. "Holy shit."

I jump out of my seat in excitement as I quickly scroll over her message, reading it.

"What!" Tori jumps up from the chair and runs over to look over my shoulder. "Is it from the bitch? She has a lot of nerve."

I squeal in excitement and hit download on the attached file. "No. It's from the author that I did the photo shoot for. She said that her cover artist sent her a mockup and that she wants me to be one of the first to view it."

"Oh wow, Calla. That is fucking awesome!" She places her chin on my shoulder and eagerly waits for the picture to load. "Can't wait to see this. Hurry!"

I shake her off and open the pictures up in my gallery. My eyes widen as I stare down at my phone. "Holy shit! Wow . . . I can't believe these are my photos. These are my photos and they're going on a book, Tori." I feel like a little kid right now as I imagine the book in my hands.

I don't even have any other words for this beauty. On the front of the cover is one of the pictures I took of Kyan in front of the white wall. He's turned sideways and his body is flexed in all the right places, looking so damn sexy. The background is now a dark, grungy looking wall with hot pink letters that read: *Before Blaine.*

The back of the cover has the blurb, along with one of the pictures of Kyan lying in his bed, only the sheet covering his deliciously firm lower body. Seeing him there, looking so damn sexy causes my heart to skip a beat as I think about what happened after these pictures.

"That is hot." Tori snatches my phone from my hand to get a closer look. "These are the photos you took? There's no way I would have been able to contain myself seeing him like *that.* These look so different than the ones I saw that one night."

I nod my head in excitement, not really hearing her words. I've never been so happy to see my work before. "Yeah. I'm speechless."

"It's amazing. This book cover deal is pretty exciting. I'm not going to lie. I'm a little jealous."

Taking my phone back, I quickly send Olivia an email before sending Kyan a message.

Me: Olivia just sent me a mockup of her cover. It looks AMAZING! You look AMAZING!

I set my phone back down, knowing that Kyan is usually busy all day, and return back to my spot on the couch. Hopefully this movie will help steer my thoughts away from Kyan for a while. Thinking about him takes my mind to places that it shouldn't be.

"Alright. Enough interruptions. Back to Ryan time."

Tori doesn't argue with that. She plops back down in her chair and hits play on the remote, starting the DVD.

We get through the first hour of the movie before someone knocks on the door. I sit up and look over at Tori, not wanting to deal with it. "Go get it. It's probably Brad."

She makes an annoyed face. "I haven't talked to Brad since this morning. He knows better than to just show up. He's a trained little puppy."

"Well get it anyways. You're closer and I'm sore."

She lets out a frustrated breath as the person knocks again. "Fine. Calm your tits, I'm coming."

She stomps across the room and over to the door. I look over the couch and watch as she opens the door to Hunter standing there. My heart does a little flip as he flashes his sexy smile.

"What the . . . Hunter?" Tori steps aside as Hunter walks in and closes the door behind him. "What the hell are *you* doing here? It's been like six years or some shit."

He walks over to the couch and plops down beside me, before grabbing my face and pressing his lips to mine. Pulling away, he smiles up at Tori. "Nice to see you again too, Tori. I was hoping Calla would join me for food and go for a ride. I need some air."

Tori gives me a very confused look, her mouth gaping open. I think I forgot to mention that Hunter lives in the same building and that we sort of slept together, or maybe I just chose not to tell her . . . because she sort of despises him.

"Hunter." I smile as I watch him lean back on the couch as if he's perfectly comfortable. I get that little giddy feeling in my stomach again, seeing Hunter sitting here on this couch like he owns the damn place. Last time he was here we were both . . . naked. "I wasn't expecting you. I mean . . . but yeah, I'm pretty hungry."

"What the fuckity fuck? I'm so damn confused right now." She looks at me wide eyed. "He just kissed you and now you're leaving Ryan for him. No one walks out on Ryan Guzman without good reason. Are you two . . . dating or some shit? Why do I not know about any of this?"

I shake my head, about to die in embarrassment if Tori keeps running her mouth. "No, we're just . . ." I have no idea how to explain to Tori that I've been sleeping with two guys. Saying it out loud just seems so . . . wrong. "Umm . . ."

"I'm just her sex slave," Hunter says teasingly. He grabs my hand and rubs it down his abs. "She can use my body whenever and for whatever she pleases."

She looks a little impressed as she fully takes in my situation. I'm sure she never would've thought in a million years that I'd have it in me to be having sex with two gorgeous men. Well, neither did I. "Wow. Didn't see that one coming." Her eyes stay on us as she walks back over to her chair and takes a seat. "He's still pretty hot as long as he keeps his mouth closed. Good fucking job."

Hunter chuckles beside me. "I'll just take that as a compliment." Grabbing my hand, he pulls me up from the couch. "I won't keep you away from this Ryan guy for long." He lifts an eyebrow in question.

I nod toward the TV. "That gorgeous guy frozen on the screen."

"Nice," he says.

Tori watches me as I grab for my purse, and I can tell she has a lot to say, but is fighting as hard as she can to keep her mouth closed. Good. Leaving with Hunter will save me some time from having to answer her endless questions about Kyan and Hunter.

"I'll be back in a bit. Pause Ryan until I get back?" I give her a sweet smile. "Please."

Tori shrugs. "I'll pause it, but only for a couple hours." She raises a brow at Hunter as he gently guides me toward the door. "Keep my friend safe. I know how you like to party. I'm sure that hasn't changed much."

"No partying," Hunter says with a smile. "Just the two of us and some good food."

My stomach fills up with knots.

Just the two of us . . .

WE STOP BY A BURGER place and get our order to- go. Hunter explained that he has a certain spot that he likes to go to be alone and just relax. He thought it'd be better than eating in a crowded place. I could agree. A little fresh air will be nice.

It feels so weird being inside Hunter's truck and I can't help but to keep looking over at him, watching him as he drives. Being with him makes me feel like I'm back in high school. I guess Hunter James will always bring back that old feeling, making me feel young again. It's weird how certain people do that.

We drive for about fifteen minutes until Hunter pulls off into the middle of nowhere and parks in the grass. It's starting to get dark, but I can easily tell that there's no one nearby. We're completely alone and the thought both excites me and has me nervous. Hunter makes me nervous.

Hunter looks over at me and smiles, all while reaching for the bag of food. "Let's eat outside. Come on." He jumps out of the truck and walks around to drop the tailgate.

I jump out after him and walk around to the back. Grabbing my hips, Hunter lifts me up and sets me on the tailgate, his hands lingering for a few seconds.

"I love eating outside." He hops into the truck beside me and digs our food out of the bag. "There's just something so peaceful about it. I hate being cooped up inside on the couch or at a table. I do that way too much."

I grab my burger and nod my head. "I agree. I'm stuck inside way more than I like." I lean my head back and smile as the breeze blows through my hair. "This is nice, Hunter."

Enjoying the night air, we both sit here in silence until we're both done enjoying our food. With bellies full, Hunter pushes the garbage out of the way and lays backward, lacing his fingers behind his head.

"I'm taking it Tori still hates me from that time I hit her with my football. That was about what . . . seven years ago?"

I lay back beside him and laugh. "Yeah, but that's Tori for ya. She isn't too fond of balls *that big* hitting her in the face if you know what I mean. You kind of overstepped her boundaries I guess."

"How about you?"

I lean up on my elbow. "Excuse me?" I laugh as he reaches

out and pulls me on top of him.

"Have I overstepped your boundaries?" He nips my bottom lip with his teeth. "Because I can't seem to keep my hands to myself."

I shake my head and rub my hand over his stomach, admiring the feel of his hard body beneath my fingers. "You're not the only one," I admit.

His eyes look down to my breasts before he licks his lips and pulls me down to kiss him. My body instantly reacts to his touch and I find myself forgetting about everything else and just enjoying the moment for what it is.

He grips my hips and grinds into me as I sit up higher, straddling him. His erection against me instantly gets me hot and I lose all train of thought as he touches me.

"I love seeing you on top of me." He pulls me toward him and kisses me again, gently tugging on my bottom lip before releasing it. "I want you to ride me right here in the back of my truck. I think it would be really fucking hot; you know, to sneak around like we all had to do in high school, having sex when and wherever we could without getting caught."

I feel a surge of excitement shoot through me at the thought, totally getting lost in his words. "That does sound *really* hot. Ironically things are so much hotter when there is risk involved." I can't help the smile that takes over my lips as he watches me move against him. I'm turning him on and I never thought that would be possible.

Before I know it, we're both fighting to get our clothes off and Hunter is reaching for a condom and slipping it on. He never seems to waste any time getting inside me. That's the difference between him and Kyan. Kyan never seems rushed. He's into pleasuring me first, while Hunter's into fucking me hard and fast. They both have me completely satisfied and wanting more. I didn't realize that was possible.

I moan out and bite my lip as Hunter lifts my hips and lowers me down to his erection. "You feel so good, Calla. I've wanted to do this for days. We can make each other feel good. Okay? Just let loose and enjoy each other's bodies. Don't hold back."

He tightens his grasp, guiding my body up and down, fast and hard. I feel him working against me each time that I come down, his thrusts bouncing me back up.

Sitting up, he grabs the back of my neck and continues to rock into me as I grind on his lap, enjoying the feel of him inside me. He feels good, but I have to admit, not as good as Kyan. The feeling is totally different and it confuses me.

"I can't believe I'm inside Calla Reynolds. Fuck me." He fists his hand in the back of my hair and slows his rhythm, making sure that I feel every single inch of him. "I seriously fantasized about this a lot in high school. No lie."

I let out a small laugh from his comment, still not able to believe that *he* wanted me. I never even thought I stood a chance. "Yeah, well it's a little hard to say no to *the* Hunter James."

He yanks my hair back, tilting my head, and runs his tongue up my neck, stopping below my ear. "Wilder," he whispers, catching me off guard.

I freeze above him, panting as I fight to catch my breath. There's no way I heard him correctly. "Excuse me?" I ask. I have to.

He pulls me closer to him and starts grinding his hips into me. "It's Hunter Wilder. James was my mother's maiden name. I had it changed as soon as I graduated."

I swallow hard and place my hands to his chest, but he just continues to rock into me, pleasuring me so good that I almost lose my train of thought.

"So Kyan . . . ?" *Please don't say it. Please don't say it.*

He pulls my face to his and looks up to meet my eyes as he thrusts harder into me and stops. "He's my older brother."

"Shit!" I get ready to get off his lap, but he stops me. "Hunter." I push against his chest in an attempt to stop him. "Kyan is the other guy that I've been sleeping with. I had no idea. This isn't right."

He lays me down flat on my back and rotates on top of me as he spreads my legs open, before pushing himself back inside of me. "I know," he whispers. "Kyan isn't capable of being in a relationship." He thrusts into me one more time and stops. "Neither am I. You deserve to be pleasured. Let us do that for you."

Hunter moving above me leaves me in a daze, unable to get my mind to work. I should be running away from this. I should be disgusted, but I'm not. I'm completely and utterly turned on. Kyan and Hunter have to be the sexiest brothers to walk this damn earth and I have the pleasure of experiencing them both. At least I can look back on this moment with no regrets, because I didn't have to miss out on either one.

I'm so wrong for this, but it feels so damn good.

"Yes . . . oh yes!" I moan out and lean my head back as he licks his thumb and rubs it over my clit, pleasuring me. "Hunter! Faster. I need you to go faster."

He moves faster and harder, biting onto my neck as I shake in his arms. "Oh shit!" He grabs my neck and starts grinding his hips. "I'm about to go. Hold on."

He thrusts a few more times before moaning and pushing off of me. His hand quickly comes down to stroke his cock and his other one goes to my left breast. "Holy fuck!" He moans, breathless.

Damn, he looks so sexy right now. I love seeing a man stroke himself. Hunter is no disappointment to that.

"That was definitely faster than I hoped it would be," he says, still working to calm his breathing. "You seem to do that to me."

I stand to my knees and grab his hips, laughing against his lips as he kisses me. "I would say sorry, but I'm guessing that's good on my part."

He brushes the hair out of my face and laughs again. "Definitely good on your part." He kisses me hard before pulling away. "Thanks for coming for a ride. It was so damn good."

I playfully slap his chest. "I really don't know what to say right now."

He reaches for his clothes and starts to get dressed at the same time that I do.

I watch him as he pulls his jeans up. "This isn't weird for you? I mean . . . I've never done anything like this before."

He pulls my face to him and softly kisses my lips. "We've never done anything like this before either, but somehow you seem to be the *exception*." He watches as I pull my shirt over my head. "I hate to rush you back home, but I have a PT session at the gym in thirty, plus I'm afraid that if I don't get you home to Ryan soon Tori is going to rip my dick off."

I get lost in my thoughts on the way home, trying to decide if this is wrong. Hunter says a few things. I just nod and pretend that I'm listening, but I can't seem to function right now.

Once we pull up at the door, Hunter gives me a quick kiss and says that he'll text me soon, before driving off. I stand outside of the building for a few minutes, looking up at the tenth floor, realizing that both men stay up there. The thought causes butterflies to fill my stomach.

When I get inside and enter the elevator, I look down at my

phone to see that I missed a text from Kyan about ten minutes ago. My emotions and thoughts are all over the place as I open it up to read it. My heart's racing.

> *Kyan: Thanks to you. ;) Just got home so jumping in the shower.*

I stand in the elevator and just stare as it opens up to the sixth floor. I can't force myself to get off, so I push the button for the tenth floor and wait for it to close.

I can't go back to my apartment without knowing how long Kyan has known about the other guy being his brother; his younger brother.

Chapter Fourteen

Calla

MY HEART IS POUNDING OUT of my chest by the time I reach Kyan's door. I have no idea how this is going to go. Somehow I feel like I did Kyan wrong. I know he told me that we're both free to sleep with other people, but I never in a million years thought that I actually would or that it would end up being his brother of all people.

I wasn't expecting Hunter to stumble into my life and I definitely wasn't expecting him to want me in the one way that I have wanted him for as long as I can remember. I feel sort of dirty right now, but a part of me still wants this.

Taking a long, deep breath, I knock on Kyan's door and stand here, tense, waiting for it to open.

The door opens a few seconds later to Kyan wrapped in a towel with water dripping from his hair and over his firm body. The sight causes me to suck in a breath. He does things to me that no one else does and I'm starting to see that. It's scary. Not even Hunter has this effect on me.

"Calla." He steps away from the door and motions for me to come inside. "Sorry. I just got out of the shower." He walks over to the fridge and pulls out two beers.

I watch as he opens both of them and extends one out for

me to grab. "That's okay," I say nervously, while grabbing the beer.

Our eyes lock as he tilts back his beer. His eyes wander over my face before he leans against the kitchen island and lets out a concerned breath. "What's bothering you, Calla? I want you to be able to say it without worry."

I walk over to stand in front of him and tilt back a few drinks for courage. "Do you know who the other guy is that I've been sleeping with?"

He stiffens with his beer touching his lips. His forehead scrunches up as he sets his beer down. "Of course I know. He's my brother, Calla. What's wrong?" He stands up, suddenly looking on edge. "Has he hurt you?"

I shake my head. "What? No." I look up into his eyes as he comes to stand directly in front of me. "So you knew this whole time that the other guy was Hunter and you never thought to tell me that he was your brother?"

He looks genuinely confused as he grabs my chin. "You said that you guys talked about us. Hunter never told you that I was his brother?"

I shake my head and try to turn away, but his grip on my chin tightens. "I would *never* lie to you, Calla. I thought he told you." He tilts his head back and bites his bottom lip in anger. "That fucking little shit."

I swallow hard as I watch him getting all worked up. "He just told me." I take a sip of my beer, trying to figure this all out. "So Hunter knew before he slept with me that you had already slept with me?"

He rubs his thumb over my bottom lip and flexes his jaw. "Yes." He steps closer to me and tangles his hands into the back of my hair. "I only let my brother be with you because I knew I had no right to tell him to back off. All that matters to me is that you're happy and pleased. I can't be that for you, so I have no right to interfere with your life." He swallows and leans down to suck my bottom lip into his mouth. "You deserve to be happy," he says against my lips. "If being with another man, whether it's my brother or someone else, makes you happy, then that's all I want. All I ask is that you stay honest with me. If you want to slap me and call me scum then go ahead." He sucks my lip again before releasing it. "Do it."

I moan as his erection pokes me through his towel. "No," I breathe. "That's not what I want. I just . . . I've never done this before and I can't figure out how to feel right now."

He leans in and runs his nose up my neck. "Then what do you want? Forget about how you *should* feel."

I say the first thing that my heart feels. "You," I whisper.

He slides his hands under my thighs and picks me up. His lips brush mine as he whispers, "Were you just with my brother?"

I nod my head, feeling ashamed. I shouldn't be doing this. I shouldn't want both of these men physically; especially brothers, but I do so damn much right now.

"Then I can't let you fall asleep thinking about him inside you." He reaches down with one hand and allows his towel to fall to the floor. "I may have let my brother have his little fun, but there's no way he's going to pleasure you better than I can."

Slamming his lips to mine, he turns around and sets me on the kitchen island, never removing his lips from mine. I push up on my hands, lifting my butt off the counter. With control, he slowly undoes my jeans and slides them down my legs. "I want to fuck you all over this apartment, Calla." He kisses me in a way that causes me to feel weak, before he pulls away and bites his bottom lip. "But first." He yanks my panties down before pulling my shirt over my head and unsnapping my bra, removing it and dropping it on the floor. "I want to fuck you against my shower wall and wash my brother off of you."

I find myself falling into him and gripping his strong shoulders as he picks me up and starts walking down the hall. "Kyan . . ." I lean back as he kisses my neck. "I don't know . . ." I breathe out heavily when I feel the head of his penis poke between my ass cheeks. "Isn't this wrong?"

"Maybe," he whispers against my neck. "But I want to pleasure you so fucking bad right now. I need to be inside you."

His lips find mine again as he opens the shower door and turns the water on. The glass door is still frosted from the shower he just got out of, and I can't help but to feel a rush knowing that we're about to have sex in his private place.

With me in his arms, he steps inside and closes the door behind him. He carefully sets me on my feet and reaches for his bar of soap. Starting at my neck, he slowly rubs it over my body, kissing the places that the water has already washed the soap off of.

He keeps getting lower and lower until his bar of soap is rubbing between my legs, his eyes level with my waist. He rubs it slowly while looking up at me. "I want to taste you . . . not anyone else." Dropping the soap, he rubs his hand between my folds, cleaning me as the water washes over my body, soaking the top of his head.

His thumb finds my clit and he looks up through wet lashes, while replacing his thumb with his mouth. I widen my stance, placing one foot on the ledge in the shower to spread myself open for him.

He runs his tongue along every inch of my pussy; so slow and torturous that I can barely stand it. Every once in a while he stops to lick his lips and wipe the water from his face, and I can't help but to take notice of how beautiful this man truly is.

His tongue starts to work faster as his finger slips between my cheeks and brushes over my asshole. I stiffen up, not used to feeling anything back there. "Kyan . . ." I moan out while gripping onto his hair. "I don't know. I . . ."

He sucks my clit into his mouth and slowly eases the tip of his finger into my hole, being sure not to give me more than I can handle. I gasp out at the mixture of feelings that takes over my body. The sensation of the tip of his finger slowly entering my ass and his tongue working over the sensitive skin of my pussy has me coming undone faster than I ever have before.

I grip his hair tighter. "Kyan! Oh yes! I'm coming!" Arching my back, I hold on tight as his perfect movements rock my orgasm right through me. He knows just what to do to make the orgasm more intense than it usually would be from any other man.

Standing up, he grips his hands into the back of my hair and kisses me mid orgasm. My mouth is open, but I immediately cling onto him as he devours my mouth just as he did my pussy.

"Did I hurt you?"

I shake my head and smile.

"Good."

Picking me up, he turns off the water and opens the shower door, stepping out. He doesn't bother to dry us off. He just walks through the house with us both dripping wet.

He stops in front of his bedroom door and kicks it open, while claiming my lips with his as if he can't get enough of my taste. I love that because I can't get enough of tasting him. I could taste him all day, every day, and never get tired of it.

"Now, I'm going to fuck you," he whispers against my lips. I'm surprised when he tosses me onto his bed, not making an effort to be gentle.

I let out a little squeal and grab onto the blanket when I land. His eyes demand mine as he slowly crawls over me and spreads my legs apart. He scoots me higher and rubs his thumb over my sensitive clit while digging in his drawer for a condom.

I start to squirm from his touch and I almost feel on the brink of another orgasm. Just watching his face and the way he looks at me is enough to make me unravel.

Once he gets the condom on, he stands on his knees and looks down at me, while grabbing my ankles, and slowly placing them on his shoulders. "Let me know if I hurt you."

He positions himself between my legs and enters me in one thrust. We both moan out as he hits hard. I don't think I've ever had a man so deep before.

He begins to move in a slow, steady rhythm before speeding up, causing me to slam my head into the headboard. I throw my hands behind me and push off of the bed as he continues to take me, hard and deep.

Watching the way his body moves above mine has me hypnotized. "I've never seen a man move his body with such beauty," I whisper.

He leans into my lips and whispers, "And I've never seen a woman as beautiful as you are, Calla. Always remember that."

His lips crush mine and I dig into his back as he pushes in deep and stops. "You feel so good inside me."

He pulls out and slams back into me again. "Better than anyone else does?" He sucks my nipple into his mouth before gripping it with his teeth. Pulling his mouth away, he looks back up at me. "Tell me."

I nod my head, telling him the absolute truth. "No one else feels this good and it scares me."

His eyes meet mine for a second as his jaw steels. I see him swallow and then before I know it, he's picking me up off the bed and carrying me through the house.

We end up in the room that we did the photo shoot in, except the walls are now painted blue and there's a white couch against the back wall, a desk and a couple tables. He walks over to the couch and sets me down on my knees, before bending me forward and shoving himself inside me from behind.

Gripping my hips, he thrusts fast and hard while rubbing his lips over my ear. The fast rhythm of his breath in my ear and the feel of him inside me has me gripping onto the couch as an orgasm washes through me, once again.

His hand reaches around, grabs the front of my throat, and pulls my neck back as he throbs inside of me, filling the condom. Once his body stills, he presses his lips against mine, kissing me gently and with passion; passion that I've never felt from him before.

A mixture of emotions cross his handsome face before he quickly shakes them off and lies back on the couch, pulling me with him.

We don't say anything. We don't have to. We're content with this moment, and right now I just want to keep it this way before I go back down to my apartment and let my shame wash through me.

I'm a horrible person for not wanting to give him up after sleeping with his brother . . .

Chapter Fifteen

Kyan

IT'S BEEN A FEW DAYS since Calla showed up at my door upset and confused about Hunter being my brother. I have to admit that it's been bothering me more than I expected and I've been finding it hard to not think about it.

When I first saw Calla at my bar a couple weeks ago, I was drawn to her beauty and her fun personality. I wanted nothing more than to see what this beautiful girl was about, knowing that I need to keep my heart in check. I thought it would be easy to be with her physically and not feel any sort of attachment, but after being with her one time and getting a taste, I knew it wasn't going to be as easy as I thought.

Then Hunter came along talking about this high school crush he had on her and I saw it as the perfect opportunity to help keep my heart at a safe distance, except this isn't how I expected to feel once he fucked her too. I expected it to make me not want her, but when she showed up at my door . . . I couldn't have been more wrong. I wanted her just as much as before, and maybe even more. That's fucked up. Now I'm starting to rethink this whole fucked up situation.

The sound of my office door opening causes me to look up from my desk. I let out a frustrated breath and grind my jaw when I see that it's Hunter.

I haven't seen much of him since he got back from vacation and seeing him now, knowing that he's been inside of Calla, rubs me wrong.

He walks over and takes a seat on the edge of my desk as if everything is perfectly normal. "Do you ever stop working?"

I pick up the stack of paperwork I was working on and shove it in my desk drawer. "Well someone's got to work around here." I look up at him and lift an eyebrow. "It's definitely not you."

He shrugs while jumping to his feet. "I work, big brother, just not as much as you do."

Looking at him right now is stirring some weird emotions inside of me. I'm usually irritated with him, so I'm used to it, but I feel irritated in the most extreme degree as I watch him standing there with his smug face.

"Why didn't you tell her before you slept with her?"

He pulls out his phone and starts typing on it. "Does it matter? She's fine with it."

Feeling pissed off as hell with his response, I knock his phone out of his hand and lean over my desk, my muscles flexed. "Yes it fucking matters. Don't you think she should've had the right to choose if she wanted to be sleeping with two brothers?" I look up at him, unable to contain my anger. He's never really taken shit seriously, but it's time for him to grow up. "You should have told her and you fucking know it. You have no idea what could be running through her head right now. The last thing she needs is to feel like shit because of us."

"She's fine." He bends down and picks up his phone, shoving it in his pocket. "What kind of girl doesn't fantasize about sleeping with two brothers and them actually be okay with it? Think about it."

I've thought about that already. Now that she knows, she might want to be with Hunter more than usual. That thought fucking stings for some reason.

"You still should have told her," I grind out. "That should have been the first thing you told her."

He walks over and grips my shoulder. His eyes meet mine and a small smile forms on his lips. "You're really worked up, bro. Just relax and enjoy her tight little pussy. It feels too good not to."

My hand reaches out to grip his neck faster than I can stop it. "Don't you fucking talk about her that way." His eyes widen as I shove him back and turn away from him.

"What the fuck." I can feel him standing close behind me, but I refuse to look at his face. I haven't been this pissed off and confused in a long time, and I don't want to end up doing something that I regret. "Are you falling for her?"

"No," I say firmly, although it somehow feels like a lie. "I'm not letting that happen again and you know it."

"You need to get over that shit, Kyan. One fucking girl screwed you over and now you act as if everyone is out to get you. Jessica was a shitty girlfriend and Bryant was an even shittier friend. Now their two kids have parents that can barely look at each other. They messed up."

"We're not talking about this shit, Hunter." I feel my blood boil just thinking about them. "I don't want to think about that shit, and I definitely don't want to think about your dick inside Calla and how it *feels* for you."

Hunter gives me an aggravated look before stalking to the door. "Well you better figure out your feelings for Calla soon before it's too fucking late. Think about that shit."

Walking out, he slams the door behind him.

"Fuck!" I sit on the edge of my desk, running both hands

over my face in frustration. Why the hell am I letting this get to me suddenly? Nothing has changed. My desire to stay unattached hasn't changed. The need to keep a safe distance hasn't changed, so why does the thought of my brother being inside Calla make me want to rip his throat out?

I get pulled out of my thoughts when my phone goes off. I recognize it right away as an LA number. I know this because I've been waiting on this call for months.

Pulling myself together, I answer the phone and make business arrangements for Kevin Goode to fly in from LA in two days to meet with me regarding the opportunity to buy his gym. This is an important deal and I want this more than anything right now.

Goode's is the biggest gym here in Chicago and the first one that started my passion of wanting to run my own gym one day. I need this deal to happen.

Chapter Sixteen

Calla

KYAN AND I FINISHED UP with our personal training session over an hour ago, but I'm still here working my ass off, not giving up until I can't walk.

We've been so caught up in sexual activities that I've been neglecting spending time at the gym. It's not as if I'm not getting a good workout at home, but . . . you know what I mean.

My legs begin to burn as I work the Elliptical faster. I'm sweating my ass off and my heart is pounding, but it feels good to work off some of this frustration.

Just as I'm about to finally stop, I feel a hand rub over my lower back. I turn beside me to see Hunter, smiling up at me. He's wearing a white shirt with the sleeves cut off and a pair of black pants. He's extremely sweaty and sexy. I don't expect him to be anything but.

"Hey, beautiful." He pulls his shirt up and wipes it over his face, soaking up the sweat. My eyes lower to his abs before back up to his face. "I just got done with a PT session. I'm about to head out if you want to leave with me."

I swallow while looking around the gym for Kyan. Last time I saw him he was walking around, encouraging and motivating his members. He stopped to push me a few times, but tried to keep it as professional as possible.

"Have you seen Kyan?" I ask breathlessly.

He smiles and nods his head as I wipe my forehead with my towel. "He's busy on the phone. It looks like he'll be in there for a while. My father always keeps him busy."

I step off the Elliptical and nod my head, while catching my breath. "Yeah, okay. I think I've had about all I can take today anyways. Let me just go say bye to Kyan."

Hunter grabs my arm and stops me from walking. "It will be better to just text him later. He didn't look too happy. Trust me."

I hesitate for a moment, feeling bad for just leaving without saying bye, but the last thing I want to do is make him even more upset than he already is.

Moving his hand up my arm, he grabs for my water bottle and walks me toward the door. "I didn't realize that you were working out here until I saw you training with Kyan." He looks up to meet my eyes as he holds the door open for me. "Kyan *never* does PT sessions, but seeing how sexual it looked, I can see why he wanted to. You seem to be his exception for a lot of things lately."

He backs me up against my jeep door and smiles against my lips, while handing me my bottle. "I'll see you in a few minutes." He presses his lips to mine, kissing me long and hard before backing away. "Don't keep me waiting." He winks and turns to walk across the lot to his truck.

Opening my car door, I hop inside and shut it behind me. "Holy shit." I run my hands over my face. "Just for fun. It's just for fun. No one is going to get hurt. Two sexy . . . oh so sexy brothers."

Once I feel that I've convinced myself, I drive off and head home, wondering what Hunter has planned.

Hunter is already waiting by an empty parking space once I pull into the back lot. He waits until I park my car before walking over and opening my door.

"Fuck, I feel as if that took forever." Leaning over me, he grabs my face and presses his lips to mine. "I want to fuck you right here, Calla."

I feel his hand slip down the front of my yoga pants and I instantly moan and throw my head back. "Hunter." I push on his head as he pulls my shirt up and quickly sucks a nipple into his mouth. "People can see us."

He releases my nipple and looks over the jeep. "No one's around right now. Everyone's at work." He bites my bottom lip. "Relax and have fun."

Pulling my legs over the side of the seat, he yanks my yoga pants and thong down and quickly pulls his hard dick out the top of his pants. He digs into his back pocket and pulls out a condom, ripping the wrapper open with his teeth.

I can't stop looking around me, checking to see if anyone's coming as he wraps my legs around him and pushes himself inside me.

"Oh shit . . . Hunter." I grab onto his hair as he grinds into me, adjusting me to his big size. "I don't want anyone to see us."

He grins and begins to thrust hard and fast. "Oh I can make it fast, baby. People might not be able to see us, but they'll be able to hear you."

Grabbing my hips, he fucks me faster and harder than he's ever moved before. I find myself biting my lip, trying to stop my screaming as he takes me.

I feel a rush from the risk of being caught as he takes me here in the open. The thought of just how public this is causes me to lose it, and I find myself clenching around him faster than

I imagined.

This causes him to smile, and he thrusts into me a few more times before pulling out, gripping the top of the jeep as he strokes himself.

"Fuck, I needed that." He pulls his condom off and shoves it in his pocket before kissing me. "Seeing you with my brother worked me up. It may be fucked up but it turned me on. I almost fucked you right there in the parking lot of the gym."

I grip onto his back as he pulls my pants up and quickly fixes my hair. "I don't think he would've liked that," I say softly, imagining how he would've felt if he caught us having sex. There's a huge difference in knowing something and witnessing it firsthand.

My heart sinks at the thought that it could possibly have some kind of affect on him.

"I need to get back to the gym." He licks his lips and smiles against my mouth. "I just had to get that out first. Glad I did too. See ya later, gorgeous."

"What the . . ." I run my hands through my hair and take a deep breath. "Hunter," I mumble.

I have no idea why I am still letting this happen. It's got to stop at some point. Right?

Nothing this easy lasts forever, at least not without someone getting hurt . . .

Chapter Seventeen

Calla

I READ MY SISTER'S LETTER for about the hundredth time, just staring at it, and letting the words blur together until my eyes begin to water. So much has happened over the last couple of weeks; more than what I'm used to. For the past two years things have been the same: work with Tori, live with Tori, and hang out with Tori. It's been simple and familiar. Now . . . now I have my sister's wedding haunting me, and two gorgeous brothers constantly running through my head, driving me insane.

Too much is happening at once and I'm beginning to feel as if I'm losing my damn mind. I need time to think. I just need to figure out these emotions that have been sweeping through me.

This all started out as fun. I was longing for something different. It was something I've never done before. Hell, I haven't even been sexually active since Jordan. It felt nice to be desired for once, but now . . . now where does this leave me? Desiring the touch of two brothers that want nothing more than a physical relationship with me? I'm so confused, but I've never been more sexually satisfied in my life.

I look up from the couch when the front door opens and closes. I hear Tori asking Brad to go to her room and wait for her, before she plops down next to me on the couch.

She nods down at the letter in my hand. "You finally read the letter, huh?"

I hold it up before flipping it over and placing it on the coffee table. "Yeah. Only once . . . or five times, but who's counting. Doesn't really matter. It's complete bullshit, but she did at least ask you to photograph her wedding. Isn't that just so damn nice of her?"

Tori squeezes the couch cushion and makes an irritated noise. "Seriously! What makes her think that I'd want to do that shit for her after what she did to you? Is she fucking high?"

I look up and face her. I can't help but to laugh at the look she's making. "Calm down before you pop an eye out. You're scaring me."

She shakes her head and lets out a deep breath to calm herself. "I'm okay. I'm okay." She takes another deep breath and releases it. "Doesn't she already have a photographer? The wedding is tomorrow afternoon."

"Yeah," I mutter. "But she said she'd rather have you. You know what she likes better than any other photographer. She's going to keep this other person booked until she hears word if you can do it or not."

"Fuck her, Calla." She grabs my shoulder and shakes me. "Get that look off your face. Don't let her bring you down. You need to show them that you're better than them, and that you've moved on." Her eyes get wide and she looks as if she's just gotten the best idea in the world. "Invite Kyan or Hunter as your date. They are both sinfully sexy and any girl would be jealous of you. One of them is way better than her stupid fiancé. Show up with one of them and show her that you came out on top."

I lean my head back and scream under my breath. She has no idea how complicated *this situation* has become. She's going to think that I'm crazy when I tell her this.

"About the boys . . ." She cocks her head, waiting for me to continue. "Apparently Hunter is Kyan's younger brother." I cover my face and shake my head, still in shock over the news. "And yes, they both know that I'm fucking them both and they don't care. It only seems to make them pleasure me harder."

Her eyes go wide and it almost sounds as if she's choking on something. "Whoa! Are you serious or are you fucking with me? You're serious?" I nod my head. "For once in my life . . . I'm speechless. I really didn't think they made brothers that damn sexy. Genes that good usually only happens once within a family."

I slap her arm, causing her to jump back and grab it. "You're not helping any here. What am I supposed to do? I haven't been with a guy in two years and now I'm having sex with two. I never planned this, Tori. It just sort of . . . hit me. "

She looks at me as if I'm stupid. "Enjoy it. Enjoy this and have your fun. It's your turn. Do you see what's happening here?"

I shake my head and reach for the letter again, rubbing it under my fingers. "This is your prize for the bad shit that you've had to deal with. It's making up for all that alone time you've spent, fluffin' your own muffin. I'm not going to lie. I would definitely jump at the opportunity to have sex with two sexy brothers. If it's not hurting anyone, then why stop? You deserve some fun in your life."

I sit here and let her words sink in. Maybe she's right. I'm not looking to jump into a relationship anytime soon, and apparently neither are the boys. Why not let us all enjoy it while it lasts. It still leaves me with one question, because I know this is something that I have to do. My father has already called me, begging me to please put the past behind me and be civil with my sister for one day. Just one day.

"Who do I ask to the wedding then?"

Tori's expression turns serious as if she didn't really take a second to consider this before. "I don't know. This is a *huge* step for you, Calla. Going to your sister's wedding is going to hurt. I'm not going to downplay it." She pauses when my eyes meet the letter. "Who can you see sitting beside you at this wedding? Who will bring you the most comfort and make it hurt less? That's who you should ask."

I look up at her as she stands up. Her words cause a whole new set of emotions to wash through me. I think about the last two weeks and how I've felt when I'm with Hunter and when I'm with Kyan. I've been trying so hard not to think too much that I've been completely blind to any feelings I've been developing.

I feel an ache in my chest as I picture his beautiful smile and the feel of his breath against my lips.

"Thanks," I whisper.

"Anytime, love." She grins and starts walking backwards. "I better get back to Brad before he starts without me. He does that sometimes."

I burst out in laughter, feeling a sense of relief for the first time in days. "Yeah. You do that. I won't keep you any longer."

An hour passes as I just sit here. I've put a lot of thought into this question, and no matter how many times I question myself my answer remains the same. The problem with that is, that this person will now have the power to hurt me. I see that now and it scares me.

I've sort of known all along, but now it's painfully clear, and if he turns down my offer to be my date at this wedding, I'm not sure I'll be able to do it alone. I don't think I can do this without him next to me.

Standing up, I shove the letter into my back pocket and make my way to the elevator before I can change my mind.

"I can do this. I can do this." I push the button on the elevator and hold my breath until it stops on the tenth floor.

The door slowly opens and I step out, mentally preparing myself for his answer.

Please don't make me do this without you . . .

Chapter Eighteen

Calla

MY HANDS ARE SHAKING WITH nerves as I reach out and lightly knock on the door. I almost feel silly, standing here about to ask him to be my date for my sister's wedding, especially since I'll be leaving early tomorrow morning. Isn't it rude to ask someone to be your date on such late notice?

I'm sure it is, Calla. Shoot!

The door opens and my heart skips a beat as my eyes land on *him.*

"Hi," I whisper.

Kyan is standing in front of me wearing nothing but black sweats, hanging so slow on his waist that you can clearly see he's not wearing anything underneath. His body is so incredibly sexy that I almost feel rude for staring, but I can't stop.

His dark hair is standing up all over the place as if he's just gotten out of bed to answer the door, and his skin is covered with a sheen of sweat.

His eyes meet mine and I notice a slight change in his breathing as his eyes lower to my mouth. "Hi." He smiles, before sweeping his tongue over his bottom lip, wetting it. "Come in."

I step inside his apartment and lean against the door as he

closes it behind me. "Did I wake you up?" I look over at the couch to see that the lamp above it is on, just giving off enough light to cover that area. A sheet is lying on the floor next to it as if it fell when he stood up.

Grabbing my hand, he pulls me close to him and places his hand on my cheek. "I don't like you standing there as if you're not welcome in my home, Calla." He places his hand on the small of my back and guides me through his living room and into the kitchen.

He turns on the light and slowly backs me into the kitchen island, before picking me up and setting me down on it. His hands are resting at the sides of my thighs as his eyes turn up to meet mine. "That's much better."

I swallow as he walks away and opens the fridge. Watching the muscles ripple in his back as he reaches for two beers causes me to have to cross my legs and wipe the palm of my hands off on my jeans.

"A beer," he questions, holding one up.

I nod my head and reach for one after he twists the cap off. "Thank you. I could actually use this way more than you can imagine right now."

He steps in between my legs and runs his hands up my thighs. "You want to talk about it?"

I take a quick sip of my beer, before letting out a small breath. "It's complicated. It's just that . . ."

I almost stop talking until his eyes meet mine and I see the sincerity in them. He's looking at me as if he truly wants to hear what I have to say. It gives me the courage to go on. "My sister is getting married tomorrow afternoon. We haven't spoken in a couple of years and seeing her get married is going to be hard, really hard."

He grips my thigh and pulls the beer out of my hand, setting it down beside me. "I'm sorry, Calla." He rubs his hands over my arms for comfort. "Are you okay?"

I shake my head and force a small smile. "Not really, but I'm trying to be."

He leans in and his lips brush mine. My heart races in anticipation of his lips meeting mine, but again . . . they don't. It causes my chest to ache with need. He presses his lips to the side of mine and runs his hands through my hair. "I'm sorry," he whispers.

My whole body shakes as he pulls away from me and takes a swig of his beer. This man is so damn beautiful that it's almost hard to believe that he's actually real.

It's getting late, and although he says that I didn't wake him up, I have a feeling that he only said it to be polite. I need to just ask him. I'm already here. I have to do this.

"I came here because I was hoping you would be my date tomorrow." He pauses from taking another drink of his beer. "I know that it's last minute, but I honestly wasn't sure that I was going until a little bit ago. It's just that . . ." I look up and meet his amber eyes, noticing him looking at me as if he can feel how nervous I am. "I don't think that I can make it through her wedding without having a date with me."

He sucks his bottom lip into his mouth, looking as if he's deep in thought. Taking one more sip of beer, he sets it down beside him and grabs my chin. "What time is it?"

My eyes scan all over his face, unable to stop looking at him. "It's at one, tomorrow. It's in Lake Geneva." His nostrils flare as he turns his gaze towards the wall. "I'm leaving early tomorrow morning around nine so that Tori can have enough time to set up her equipment. It's okay if you don't want to go."

"I want to go." He turns back to face me with a look of disappointment on his face. "But I can't." He takes a step back and lets out a frustrated breath. He seems torn. "I have an important meeting tomorrow at noon. It's a big opportunity for me . . ." He trails off while running his hand through his hair. He almost looks pained as he speaks again. "Have you thought about asking Hunter?"

I shake my head and jump down to my feet. "No. I wanted to ask you." I offer him a smile and start heading for the door. "It's not a big deal. It will be over before I know it."

I feel his hand on the small of my back as I reach for the door handle. "I know this doesn't offer much help, but you can text me during the wedding if it helps. I'll be sure to keep my phone in my lap."

I stop at the door and turn around to face him. "Thanks, but tomorrow is important for you. Don't worry about me. I'll be fine." Returning his favor, I grab the back of his head and press my lips to the side of his mouth.

I hear a small gasp escape his lips as I pull away and turn for the door.

"Goodnight, Kyan."

"Goodnight, Calla," he whispers back, before I close the door and walk away.

I'm going to have to do this on my own . . .

Chapter Nineteen

Kyan

I'M DUE TO MEET Kevin Goode in thirty minutes at his office. I'm usually never nervous, especially when it comes to deals that I know I'll have no problems closing, but I'm definitely feeling on edge today.

My mind keeps going back and forth between thinking about this deal for the gym and thinking about how Calla has to face today on her own. I just can't seem to get past the hurt I saw in her eyes last night when I told her I couldn't make it. She tried to hide it, but it was clear as day.

Straightening my tie, I grab my wallet and shove it into my pocket while making my way into the kitchen. I open the fridge, pull out a bottle of water, and get ready to open it, when I notice the corner of a white piece of paper, sticking out from under the kitchen island.

Curious, I pick it up and quickly unfold it to see that it's addressed to Calla. I almost fold it back up and get ready put it back down, but my damn curiosity gets the best of me.

Swallowing, I read over the letter.

Calla,

I know that it's been a while. It's been a little over 2 years to be exact. I've tried numerous times to reach out to you, but after being repeatedly shut down, I've given up. I apologize for that. I know that I hurt you and it should be on me to keep trying until you forgive me, but I didn't. I'm not as strong as you. I never have been. That's why when I started having feelings for Jordan, I couldn't shut them off and walk away. The thing that kills me every day is that I know you would have been able to if the roles were reversed. You may not think that I'm hurt by that day when you walked in on Jordan and me, and that it doesn't haunt me still to this day, but it does. I'm sorry, so very sorry, but you can't stop love. Love is a force that cannot be controlled. I know it might hurt for you to read this, but I love Jordan more than I love life. If I didn't . . . then I wouldn't be marrying him, but I also love you. You may not believe me at the moment, but I do. That's why I want you there. I don't expect you to be my maid of honor or a bridesmaid or to even watch me walk down that aisle, but just knowing that you're here for my special day will be enough. Please, please, please think about it before saying no.

Love your sister,

Chrissy Reynolds.

The letter falls out of my hand as I run my hands over my face and clench my jaw. My chest aches at the thought of Calla having to go through this bullshit. It fucking hurts on a personal level. Now I see why she was so torn about going today. I know more than anyone what it feels like to be hurt by two people that you love. I'm still living in the pain to this fucking day.

I walk around in a fucking daze as I repeat the letter in my head. I should be leaving right now. I should be out that door, but I can't bring myself to leave.

"Fuck. I'm so sorry, Calla." I freeze mid stride and slowly rub my hands down my face. I'm standing here, lost in my own thoughts, until my phone vibrates in my pocket.

I pull it out to see a message from Kevin Goode.

> *Kevin: I only have a limited amount of free time so please be sure to be here at our scheduled time. This is a one-time opportunity, Mr. Wilder.*

I tug on my tie, suddenly feeling as if I can't breathe. I need to go before it's too late.

A one-time opportunity . . .

Grabbing my keys, I rush out the door and run to the elevator. I continue to push the button until the elevator doors swing open in front of me. I stop and look at Jessica standing before me, my heart completely stopping in my chest. It's been three years since I have seen her and now here she is in front of me, looking as if she wants nothing more than to throw her arms around me and cry.

She steps out of the elevator and looks me up and down. "Kyan . . ." She gets ready to hug me, but I put my arm out stopping her. "I'm sorry. It's just been so long," she says.

I grind my jaw and watch as she plays with the strap of her purse. "What do you want, Jessica? I really don't have time right now."

Looking at her, I can't help but to notice how good she looks. She looks just as beautiful as the day I fell in love with her: long, red hair, little freckled nose, and the longest legs I've ever had the pleasure of touching. That used to be my favorite thing about her . . . until I found out she was wrapping them around my best friend when I was away on a business trip.

"I miss you." Her big blue eyes meet mine and I can see the truth in them. There's no denying the pain in her eyes right now. You'd have to be blind not to notice. "I was hoping we could talk. I know that we can't just work things out over night or even after a week, but I want a chance to start over. I love you, Kyan, and I've never stopped."

Shaking my head, I give her a good long look and realize what I've been missing all along; the one fact that I've been denying to myself over the years. "I don't love you anymore," I say. I don't even realize that I'm saying the words out loud until she covers her mouth and tears roll down her cheeks. "Go take care of your kids, Jessica. Forget about me, and what we had. Give Bryant a fucking chance, because *we* will never be together again. You had the chance to be my wife, but it wasn't meant to be. I've spent years hurting over you, but I'm done . . ."

I step into the elevator and hit the button. "I have to go. Tell Bryant I said hi."

"No, please." She reaches her hand out to stop the elevator. "Kyan . . . think about this. We could be together just like old times."

I let out a stupefied laugh, not believing my fucking ears. "Yeah. You, me, and your two kids that you have with my *best friend.* You just had to have him then, well now you do. Wake up, Jessica. Have a good life."

The elevator door closes and I smile at the huge sense of relief that washes over me. I have refused to see Jessica since our split, but seeing her just opened my fucking eyes. We were minutes away from walking down the aisle last time I laid eyes on here. It blinded me, but the truth is I haven't loved her in a long time. It was the betrayal that hurt me more than losing her, and that's something I need to never fucking forget.

Ten floors have never seemed so fucking long before. I feel as if this is the longest elevator ride of my damn life as I ride it down to the first floor.

The elevator doors open and I immediately step out, walking at a steady pace until I'm outside and heading toward the back parking lot.

Stopping for a second to compose myself, I open the door to my Mercedes and calmly get inside, shutting the door behind me. "Take care of business, Kyan."

I sit here, squeezing my steering wheel, trying to figure out things in my head, before starting the engine and taking off.

I have to do this. I can't force myself not to . . .

Chapter Twenty

Calla

THE PARK IS SO BEAUTIFUL that it causes an ache in my chest, as I look around at all the scattered flowers below my feet. My sister has always loved lilies and now they're everywhere I look. There's no escaping them or this.

I refused to show up too long before the wedding, so I had Tori drop me off at the hotel and take the car so she could set up. My father picked me up about twenty minutes ago and I have been trying in every way possible to ensure I don't run into Chrissy. I'm here. That's enough for now. I'll have to ease into the rest.

The ceremony is due to start in ten minutes, so I'm walking around by the water, waiting for everyone to take their seats. Of course, Chrissy reserved a special spot for me in the front row, so I have no choice but to sit there and feel awkward, especially since I won't have Tori next to me.

I've gotten glimpses of Jordan from afar, but I've been trying to block that image from my head. That jerk doesn't deserve my heartache. He meant everything to me. I loved him with everything in me and he promised me that he did in return. We met during my senior year and we became inseparable. I actually thought that he was *the one;* the one that I would start a family with and live happily ever fucking after with. Boy was I wrong . . . so wrong.

Walking in on Chrissy riding Jordan's dick as if she needed it to survive will always burn in the back of my brain, ripping my heart out. That is an image that you *never* get rid of, no matter how many times you fight it. Trust me. I've tried and failed miserably. I mean who the fuck cheats on his girlfriend with her sister and then marries her?

"Hey, Calla . . . wait up."

My heart skips a beat and I stand frozen on the spot at the familiar sound of Jordan's voice. I haven't heard it in years, and hearing it now almost feels as if no time has passed. The sound is like a knife twisting in my damn heart. I hate it!

I hear his footsteps behind me, before I feel his hand grab my arm. "Calla. Can I have a second? Please."

Swallowing back my emotions, I pull my arm out of his reach and stiffen my arms at my sides. I don't want his hands anywhere on me. The thought disgusts me. I can't even look at him, so I give him my backside as I speak. "What do you want, Jordan? You're getting married in less than ten minutes. No need to waste your time on me."

"Calla . . ." He lets out a small breath and I feel his body almost touching me from behind, but he stops, not letting himself get too close. "I just want to thank you for coming. It means more to your sister than you could ever imagine. She was so afraid . . ."

I spin around and face him, cutting him off. "What, Jordan? Afraid that I wouldn't come watch her happily ever after happen? The two people that meant the most to me in the world that betrayed and hurt me? Was she afraid that I wouldn't suffer through it so I can see how happy and in love you two are? Huh? Is that what she was afraid of?" Seeing his face up close makes me feel nauseous.

His eyes widen and I see him swallow nervously as he looks behind me, over my shoulder. Good. Someone's watching. I don't care who the hell sees my little outburst. They can watch from afar, because I've been holding this in for years.

He takes a quick breath and releases it. "No. Calla. That's not . . ."

"I gave you everything I had, all of me." I point to my chest with my hand shaking. I'm so angry that it's uncontrollable. I don't want him to see the way it's affecting me, but it can't be stopped so fuck it. "I loved you, Jordan. I cherished you and listened to you . . . I took care of you. I did everything that I was supposed to do and it still wasn't good enough for you. You ripped my fucking heart out and stomped on it, and with who . . . huh? The most important person in my life next to you, my sister. My fucking sister, Jordan. You did that to me. Not only did you rip my fucking heart out, but you also stole my family. That's something you don't come back from. You can't just pretend it's all okay just because two years has passed."

His jaw clenches and his eyes look over my shoulder again, as he runs a hand through his short, blonde hair; his stupid, always perfect hair. "I'm sorry. I can't take that back and neither can she. You think we meant for it to happen that way?"

"I don't care. It should've never happened in the first place. If you two wanted to be together . . . then you should have told me. I loved you both enough that I would have backed off and gave you the space to figure it out, because that's my character. What's sad is that you know that, but instead you both betrayed my trust in the worst way possible. How do you expect me to trust my heart with anyone else after the two people I loved the most completely fucked it up by shredding it into a million pieces?" I tilt my head up to meet his brown eyes. "It still fucking hurts. Just thought you both should know."

I hear footsteps right behind me, crunching in the grass, before I feel a hand possessively lace with mine, causing me to release a surprised gasp.

Turning my eyes away from Jordan, I look beside me to see Kyan, looking straight ahead at Jordan as if he's mentally ripping his throat out.

My heart literally skips a fucking beat and a tear slowly trails down the left side of my face as I stare at him in awe. I can't believe that he's standing here, next to me. I'm so happy that I could die right now. When I needed him the most he came through.

He's dressed in a pair of form fitting trousers and a white button down shirt, with the sleeves rolled up to the elbows. His tie is loose as if he's been pulling on it, but his hair is slicked back as if he actually took the time to style it before arriving. He looks so painfully sexy and I can tell that Jordan notices it too. I'm sure Jordan's used to being the sexiest guy everywhere he goes. Too bad for him he won't be for his own damn wedding.

"Sorry I'm late, Calla." His eyes stay straight ahead on Jordan's and I can easily tell that Jordan feels extremely uncomfortable as Kyan sizes him up. His eyes keep darting from my face to Kyan's face, and then to our hands laced together. "Let's go find our seat and let the groom here get married."

His jaw steels as Jordan loosens his tie. Then, before I know it, his hand is on my lower back and he's guiding me through the grass and toward where Jordan *should* be right now.

Going back to holding my hand, he walks me down the aisle as if it's perfectly normal for people to be looking at us as if we're a real couple. I see my aunt fan her face off and grin as Kyan pulls me past her toward the empty seat in the front row.

There's only one seat open together, so Kyan leans in and politely asks someone that I don't know if they wouldn't mind moving over to the next seat so that we can sit together.

My stomach fills with butterflies as he guides me down to my seat and takes a seat beside me, pulling my hand into his lap.

His fingers trace circles on my hand and I oddly find comfort in his touch, as I look straight ahead, ready for this to be over.

The soft music starts and I feel Kyan move my chair as close to his as he possibly can. It causes a small smile to take over my lips as I watch him looking at me. He's taking me all in as if he's making sure that I'm okay.

"Thank you," I whisper. "You didn't have to do this."

His jaw muscle flexes as he nods his head. "Yes, I did," he says barely above a whisper.

My heart races as I take notice of the first couple making their way down the aisle to stand at the front. This is all so real now. It's actually happening right in front of my eyes. My sister is marrying Jordan . . . my first and only love.

Sitting here right now, watching this, is one of the hardest things I've ever had to do. With each second that passes I feel sicker to my stomach from the anticipation of seeing Chrissy walk down that aisle.

Kyan's hand squeezes mine, comforting me as Jordan makes his way down the aisle to take his place.

He seems to know how much this hurts and I couldn't be more thankful to have him here with me. I owe him so much for this and I can never repay him enough. He's giving up something important for him to be here right now. No one has ever done anything like that for me before.

The music changes and my whole body stiffens. I rub my

free hand over the front of my silver, silk dress, as my nerves begin to get the best of me. She's only seconds away from walking down that aisle and I know for a fact that she will be looking to see if I actually made it.

I sit a little higher, unable to hide like I know I should. For some reason I desperately want to see her. I almost need to. I don't want to talk to her and pretend that everything is okay, but I just want one look at my beautiful sister after so much time has passed. It's been too long.

Oh my God . . .

There she is looking more beautiful than she did two years ago. Her long, blonde hair is twisted into a braid and clipped in a side bun, with little flowers sticking out, and her dress is the most beautiful thing I have ever laid eyes on. She truly is a beautiful bride, and seeing her causes my heart to swell with unwanted pride.

I see her looking my way, trying to spot me out. Her eyes meet mine and I see her suck in a breath as if she's about to cry. It causes me to almost have a breakdown. I find myself squeezing Kyan's leg so hard that my nails are probably digging into his skin through his pants, but he allows me to do it without complaint.

Our eyes stay locked, taking each other in, until they can't anymore. This is so hard. God, I love her so much. I'm starting to lose it and I don't want anyone to see me burst into tears.

I start to shake as the unwanted tears fill my eyes. The priest is talking, but I can't concentrate on any of his words. I feel as if I'm about to break into a sob at any second.

"It's okay." Kyan grabs my face with both hands and forces me to look him in the eyes. "Look at me, okay. Keep your eyes on me. There's no one here but the two of us."

I nod my head and speak through my tears. "Okay," I whisper.

His eyes keep mine captured as the rest of the world goes on around us. It's as if we're taking this moment to read each other and really see what the other is feeling.

His face looks pained as if he's carrying my hurt. It suddenly makes me ache for him and not for myself anywhere.

He must notice my change in emotion because his eyes bounce back and forth between mine, before he wraps his hand into the back of my hair and pulls me in for a kiss.

When his lips meet mine, my whole world stops, and I feel as if I'm melting into him. He's never kissed me outside of sex before and it definitely has my emotions running wild. This is new for him.

His lips move with mine as if he's lost in me and he wants nothing more than to own me with this kiss . . . and he does. This one kiss owns me, along with my heart.

The feel of his tongue sweeping across my bottom lip causes flutters in my stomach. His kiss is so gentle, yet filled with so much passion that I feel breathless in his embrace.

He pulls away and rubs his thumb over my check, leaving me utterly speechless. "You look beautiful," he whispers. "So damn beautiful that I'm feeling things I haven't felt in a long time."

My heart swells from his words and I find myself gripping onto his hands as he holds my gaze, being sure I don't have to witness the worst part of it all. He's got my complete attention, and to be honest, no one else can capture it quite like he does. I could sit here and look into his eyes forever and never get tired of trying to figure them out.

Before I know it people are starting to stand around us and we're the only ones still sitting here just staring at each other.

I swallow and pull away from his eyes to see that the wedding party is preparing to walk back down the aisle. Everyone is now standing proudly to watch Chrissy and Jordan take their final walk hand in hand as husband and wife.

My eyes fall on my sister as she makes her way down the aisle. The first thing I notice are the tears of joy on my sister's face. She truly looks as if her dream has just come true, her happily ever after. Her eyes go from looking at Jordan to seeking me out.

She notices Kyan and me together, and a huge smile appears on her face as she nods at me and then continues to pass. That one little smile is almost enough to break through my wall and make me want to run to her, but I don't.

Wow . . . it doesn't even feel like five minutes have passed when in reality it's been at least twenty, and Kyan's eyes didn't leave my face once.

Grabbing my hand, Kyan stands up and helps me to my feet. He slips an arm around my waist and presses his lips to the side of my forehead as we wait for a clear exit.

We stand here as each row of people makes their way outside and lines up with bubbles before Kyan walks me down the aisle and outside.

He grabs a thing of bubbles and hands it to me. "Do you want to do this? You don't have to. Don't push yourself if it hurts too much."

Deciding that I need to be strong, I take the bubbles and begin to open the cap while nodding my head. Seeing Chrissy and Jordan walk down the aisle, happily in love, has made me realize how much time has truly passed between us and I'm beginning to question if it was all worth it.

It's also made me realize that what I felt for Jordan is completely gone. I feel nothing but anger when I look at him. It's my anger that has kept me away for so long, not a broken heart from the loss of Jordan like I thought.

Looking at Chrissy gives me a feeling of loss and pain. It's family that truly matters. It's losing her as my sister that hurts the most. I need to let go and learn to let her in again. I've been weak and it's time that I stand up straight and be strong for the both of us. It's just going to take time to truly forgive her.

Kyan stands behind me and wraps his arms around my waist as I begin blowing bubbles at the newlyweds when they pass. Having him nearby seems to make things easier. He gives me that sense of peace that I've been seeking.

He's managed to be my peace through the hardest thing I've ever had to do in my life . . .

AFTER THE CEREMONY KYAN HELPED pack up Tori's equipment and then unpack it again once arriving at the reception.

Tori mostly stood back with a grin on her face and watched him do the work, but you get what I mean. As soon as she noticed me standing around with Kyan, she practically screamed. Her words were, "I knew he'd show up."

That's crazy, because I had no idea. I still honestly cannot believe that he is here right now. I can't stop looking at him and smiling. He notices and smiles back each time, looking as if he's the happiest man on earth.

Right now, he's standing by the bar chatting with my father. I see them both casually look my way and I can't help the nerves that shoot through me. I have no idea what they're discussing, but they both look extremely happy.

Smiling, my father pats Kyan on the back before shaking his hand and walking away. My sister and Jordan just arrived a few minutes ago, so I'm sure he's making his way to see them.

I look up and reach out for the glass of wine as Kyan hands it to me. "Thank you." I quickly tilt the glass back and finish it off.

Kyan raises an eyebrow. "Isn't the point of wine to sip and savor? Should I just buy the whole bottle now and save me some trips? I will buy you the whole bar if it helps." He smirks and then pulls me to him, sucking the excess wine off my bottom lip. "Mmm . . . tastes delicious."

I laugh as he leans back in and teasingly nibbles my bottom lip. "Kyan . . ."

"Sorry," he smiles against my lips. "You taste too damn good."

"Calla . . ." My heart stops and all of my oxygen escapes me as Chrissy's voice comes from right behind me. "Can I have a minute, please?"

Kyan grabs my face with both hands and rubs my cheeks as I look up at him. "I'll find you in a bit." He leans in and kisses me softly on the lips, before walking away, leaving me alone with . . . Chrissy.

Closing my eyes, I take a deep breath and slowly release it. When I open my eyes again, I see Tori across the room, watching me. She gives me a slight smile and nods her head. I guess her being here has somewhat opened her eyes as well.

I turn around to face Chrissy and her soft eyes land on my face, taking me all in. "I'm really happy you came." She swallows nervously and reaches for my hand. My eyes look down at her hand holding mine, before looking back up to her face. "There are things that need to be said. I can't hold them in anymore. I'm so sorry, Calla. I know I can't make up for what

I did, but I'll try if you'll let me." Her hand squeezes mine as a tear slides down her cheek. "I miss you."

Fighting back my sob, I squeeze her hand back. "I miss you too," I admit.

"I didn't mean to hurt . . ."

"Let's not do this here," I say, cutting her off.

My eyes wander off when I hear the refreshing sound of Kyan's laugh. He's standing next to my aunt and a small group of older women. I can't help the smile that takes over as I watch him having fun. That's what weddings are supposed to be: fun and happy . . . not this.

Nothing else seems to matter at the moment but the fact that he's here, supporting me. The past doesn't matter. The anger that I've held onto for so long . . . it doesn't matter. Maybe it's just time to leave everything behind.

Smiling, I reach out and touch my sister's face. "We don't need to talk about this anymore. I love you and I want you to be happy. It's going to take a while to fully gain my trust, but I want you in my life. Baby steps, okay?"

Crying, Chrissy leans in and throws her arms around me, nearly squeezing me half to death. She holds me, smiling against my cheek. "That's all I want."

She pulls away and tugs on a strand of my hair. "You look so beautiful. Your hair has gotten so long." She nods her head toward Kyan. "And that handsome man looks extremely happy to be with you. You deserve that happiness. Don't push it away, okay?"

We both look over at the same time that Kyan turns to face us. He flashes us a dimpled smile as Aunt Sharon pulls him out onto the dance floor.

"Oh no." I give Chrissy one last quick hug. "You're an absolutely beautiful bride, but I have to go save Kyan. You know how Aunt Sharon gets."

"Oh definitely." She smiles and shakes her head as my aunt's hands start to rub Kyan's lower back. "You better hurry. She's working faster than usual."

Laughing, I hurry across the room and place my hand on Sharon's back. "This one is mine, you old hussy."

We both crack a smile at the same time before she releases Kyan and steps away. "I was hoping your sister would keep you busy long enough for me to cop a feel." She winks. "Enjoy this one." She wiggles her penciled in brows and then walks away, looking for her next victim.

Kyan wets his lip and quickly pulls me against him. "Is this you returning the favor for me coming? You saving me from that innocent woman?"

I stand up on the tip of my toes and laugh against his lips. If only he knew. "No . . . my repaying you for coming would definitely involve you coming." I smirk as he bites his bottom lip and pulls it into his mouth. "You look incredibly sexy in that suit," I whisper.

He slides his hand beneath my neck and dips me backward, placing his lips to my ear. "And that dress makes me want to rip it off of you and fuck you incredibly long and hard. I'm trying my best not to fuck you right here on the dance floor."

Pulling me back up, he wraps both hands in the back of my hair and grinds against me to the music.

"Oh damn!" Tori appears beside us and starts snapping pictures as Kyan continues to move against me. "You two need to find a bathroom or some shit and stop teasing the rest of us." She laughs and snaps a few more pictures while backing away.

"She's right," Kyan says against my lips. "We need to find a bathroom, because I need to be inside of you. Now."

Grabbing my hand, he pulls me through the room, smiling and nodding as random people greet us. Once we get out into the hallway, he holds me up against the wall and slides his hands up my dress.

His lips meet mine and he kisses me so deeply that my body trembles in his arms. "I need you, Kyan . . ." I tug at his tie, nipping his bottom lip with my teeth. "I need you inside me. Now."

Kyan smirks before grabbing my hand and pulling me away from the wall to look for an open bathroom. He pulls me down a side hall where no one's at and dips into the first unlocked bathroom, locking it behind us.

His hands find my thighs and he picks me up, wrapping my legs around his waist with such force that my breath gets knocked out of me.

Not able to hold back, I tangle my fingers in his thick hair and crush my lips to his. He slams me against the wall and then the stall, before finally setting me down on the sink, pulling my dress up my thighs.

"Damn, I'm so fucking hard." He grabs my hand and places it on his erection. "Only you get me this hard, Calla."

Sliding my panties down my legs, he runs his lips along my skin, teasing me on the way. Standing back up, he tosses my thong aside and steps between my legs.

Smirking, he grabs my neck and pulls me to him, brushing his lips over mine. "I wish I had more time to pleasure every inch of your body, but that will have to wait till later."

I watch in wonder as he quickly undoes his pants and zipper, before pulling his incredibly hard dick out, stroking it while looking me in the eyes.

I start grinding my hips to get closer to him, just wanting him inside me already. Watching him stroke himself is pure torture. I'm extremely jealous of that hand right now.

He brushes his thumb over my bottom lip, causing me to lean into his touch. "Are you on the pill, Calla?" His jaw tightens as he watches me, waiting for an answer.

My insides do a little flip at the thought of him going bare inside me. I've never had sex without a condom. Jordan always made sure we used one. This is new and very . . . very hot.

I nod my head and wrap an arm around his neck, pulling him to me. "Yes, so just fuck me already. I want you, Kyan."

"Shit, I love your mouth." Without hesitation, he wraps my legs around his hips and slams into me. We both moan out at the feel of him naked inside of me. My insides shiver from the rush that it gives me.

"Oh shit, Kyan . . ." I smile against his lips. "No one has ever been inside me like this before."

He grips my face and forces me to look him in the eyes. "Never?"

"Never," I whisper. "Only you."

Before I can even take another breath, he has me off the sink with my back pressed against the bathroom door.

The door bounces against the frame as he thrusts into me, fucking me deep and hard, being sure that I feel every inch of him inside me . . . and I do. I feel it all right. I feel it like I've never felt anything before.

His lips devour my lips, tasting me and teasing me like never before. The movement of his hips and the feel of his strong arms holding me have me completely satisfied and ready to surrender myself to him whenever he pleases. He's that good and he knows it.

He's taken the time to make sure that I'm always pleased and sex with Kyan only seems to get better each time.

Gripping my neck, he slows his movement, grinding his

hips into me as his breath fans my lips. He's grinding his hips so slow, and with perfect rhythm, that it reminds me of when we were dancing on the dance floor.

"Oh my God . . . Kyan." I grip onto his hair and slam my head into the door as he quickens his pace, hitting my spot every single time. "I love you inside me," I whisper. "So deep."

He thrusts hard, then stops. "I only want me inside you like this, Calla." He thrusts again, causing me to scream out and squeeze him with my legs. "Only my cock."

I nod my head, lost in the moment. "Okay." I bite my lip as he looks into my eyes. "Okay."

That one words causes him to lose it. Gripping my face, he pounds into me, not slowing down until I'm coming undone and screaming in his arms.

A few seconds later, he carries me to the sink and sets me down as he quickly pulls out of me. He reaches for his dick and strokes it a few times, about to come any second, but I quickly push his hand away and jump down to my knees. I want to taste him so bad that my chest aches.

Swirling my tongue around the head of his dick, I suck it into my mouth while stroking it with my hand. A few seconds later I feel his cum hit the back of my throat. Without even thinking about it, I swallow it, being sure to clean up every last drop afterwards.

He throws his head back and moans, watching me with the biggest smile I've ever seen on him. Reaching for my hand, he pulls me up to my feet and presses his forehead to mine. "I think I'm in love," he teases.

My heart swells for a split second until I quickly remind myself that he didn't mean it like that.

We're standing here, looking each other in the eyes, when someone knocks on the door. We both just smile as he helps me put myself together before fixing himself.

The person knocks again. "Any day now."

"Coming," Kyan says with a smirk.

I burst out in laughter before playfully pushing his chest. "I guess it's only polite to get back to the wedding and give this asshole the bathroom."

Grabbing my face, Kyan bites my bottom lip before sucking it into his mouth. "That's okay. We have all night afterwards."

I tilt my head and look at him in question. "We do?"

He nods his head and smiles, the cutest damn smile in the world. "I booked a room on the way here. You're staying with me and Tori is driving back to Chicago." He places his hand on my lower back. "Let's go."

I smile and walk out of the bathroom with pride, as Kyan holds the door open for us. To my surprise, Jordan is leaning against the wall waiting to get in. I was so wrapped up in Kyan that Jordan's voice didn't mean shit. It was a stranger to me.

He walks past us, giving us an awkward head nod, before closing himself into the bathroom.

Walking back to the party, all I can think of is how Kyan booked a room and wants me to stay with him. He couldn't even kiss me on the mouth and *now* he wants me sleeping in the same bed as him.

I'm not sure I can survive a night with Kyan Wilder . . .

Chapter Twenty-One

Kyan

BEING HERE FOR CALLA BECAME my top priority for the night. I'm well aware that I fucked up with Kevin and I won't be getting my gym, but there comes a time when you need to realize that the people you care about are more important. There will be other fucking gyms. There won't be another Calla.

The look in her eyes and reading that letter tore at me. Then when I saw Jessica, I realized that just because it was easier for me than I expected, doesn't mean it would be as easy for Calla; especially when it involved seeing both people that hurt her getting married. I couldn't let her go through that alone.

The party ended over thirty minutes ago, so I left Calla downstairs in the lobby to say goodbye to her family. When she gets up here I plan to spend the night making sure that she feels good. I won't let her be unhappy while she's here in my arms. I may not be able to offer her much at home, but tonight I can.

The door opens as I'm pulling my shirt and tie off. I bring my attention up to Calla and smile. "How did it go?"

She shamelessly checks out my chest and abs as I stand here running my hands through my hair. Smiling, she falls back on the bed and grabs the blanket. "It went as well as it could, I suppose. It's not going to be easy, but Kyan . . ." She grabs my hand and pulls me toward the end of the bed. "You made it so much less painful. I can never thank you enough for coming. What about that meeting you had?"

I crawl onto the end of the bed and scoot her up towards the headboard. Taking off her heels, one by one, I toss them beside me on the floor. "It's not a big deal. There will be more meetings in my future."

She closes her eyes and releases a satisfied breath as I massage her legs, slowly working my way up to her thighs. "Kyan, your hands feel so good." She bites her bottom lip as I massage right under her ass cheeks. "I could let you do this all night. Oh wow."

A laugh rumbles deep in my chest as I lean over and pull her dress over her head. "Well, we have all night and my hands definitely never get tired of touching you." Slowly, I pull her up and unsnap her bra, letting it fall to the bed beside us. Then I go down in between her legs and grab her thong in my teeth, slowly pulling them down her legs.

My hands rub her legs on the way down, massaging over her soft, smooth flesh. She arches her back and lets out a small moan while watching me. "You do something to me, Kyan."

I run my hands all the way up her body, applying pressure until I reach her breasts. Then I massage them soft and slow, while running my lips up her neck. "You do something to me too," I admit. "More than I ever expected you to."

Reaching her mouth, I press my lips against hers, claiming her lips as mine. They may not belong to me, but for tonight they do, and I plan to make sure she knows that.

Sitting up so I can reach my pants, I undo them and slip them down my thighs, before standing up and kicking them to the side. I reach out for her hand and place it on my stomach as I remove my boxer briefs next.

I'm standing here completely naked, my body hers to do with whatever she pleases. I don't care if she wants to fuck me or just look at me. My dick doesn't get to choose tonight. She does. This is all about her.

Spreading her legs, I slowly crawl above her and grab for the bottle of hotel lotion that I found lying around in the bathroom. I open the cap before squirting it into my hands and rubbing them together.

She looks up at me, completely lost in me as she watches me make my way down her body, massaging the lotion up her right leg. I work on that leg for a few minutes before moving to the next leg and working that one just as good.

"Kyan," she says, completely relaxed. "Why did you choose to come to the wedding instead of your meeting?"

I position myself between her spread legs and gently rub my hands up her stomach and sides.

My situation with Jessica and Bryant isn't something that I usually talk about with others, but knowing that she's been hurt the same, I really don't have a choice. She needs to know that I understand her pain and while we're here tonight, I'm willing to ease it the best way I know how.

She sucks in a breath as my cock brushes her entrance. I'm fully hard right now, and with the most beautiful woman I've ever seen lying naked beneath me. This isn't exactly the ideal time to talk about this but . . .

"I know how you feel," I say stiffly. Her eyes meet mine and widen in curiosity. "To make a long story short, I found out not long before I was about to walk my fiancé down the aisle that she was pregnant with my best friend's baby." I pause and swallow. "I found your letter, Calla. I couldn't let you go through this alone, knowing how it feels to get fucked over like that."

I feel her squeeze my arm as her bottom lip begins to tremble. She's fighting hard to stop it, but it's not working. "Bryant had been my best friend for over ten years and Jessica was my first real love. I went away on a business trip for a few weeks when I was looking into buying my own gym for the first time, and then she found out she was pregnant three weeks later. We were about to get married and Bryant freaked out and confessed that he was in love with Jessica and that she was carrying his child, so I ended our engagement and gave her and Bryant the house I owned. They had a baby coming, so they needed it more than I did. It was the worst year of my fucking life."

I bring my eyes up to meet hers and I can see the pain in them as she watches my face. "I'm so sorry." She kisses my arm. "Are they still together?"

I nod my head and huff. "Yeah. They have two kids together, but they aren't happy. I feel sorry for the kids." I shake my head and grab her face to comfort her. "Let's not worry about that tonight. Okay? I just want to make you feel good."

Her jaw tightens as her eyes meet mine. "Then make love to me," she whispers. "Let me feel you."

Swallowing back the emotions that her words bring, I slide my hand under her neck and gently guide myself between her legs. I slowly push into her, moaning as her tightness hugs me completely.

Her body moves with mine, her nails digging into my back as I slowly grind my hips, being sure to hit every spot of pleasure I can find. Hearing her moan and feeling her grip on me tighten pushes me to want to pleasure her even more.

Being inside her this way feels too good emotionally and physically, and I can't help but to feel selfish and only want it to be me from now on.

As I push into her I can't help but to be haunted by my

thoughts of my brother inside her, but I quickly fight the anger and jealously off and make love to her like she truly deserves.

Bringing her legs over my shoulders, I slightly lift her hips and rock into her, biting the side of her calf as I bury myself as deep as I can.

Both of our bodies are covered in sweat. We're both breathless and completely lost in each other as I continue to thrust deep and slow for what feels like hours.

Wanting to be closer to her, I sit on my knees and bring her body up to straddle my lap. Our bodies are plastered together, not even an inch of breathing room as I kiss her flesh all over and bury myself inside her.

I feel her nails dig into my skin and her breathing picks up next to my ear. "I want to come with you, Kyan. I can feel that I'm getting close."

Holding her as close as possible, I press my lips to hers and sway my hips, pulling her body so I can get as deep as I can. I feel myself close to orgasm so I suck her bottom lip into my mouth, moaning as she clenches around my cock.

A few seconds later, I rock into her one last time, releasing my load inside her, being sure that she gets every last drop.

She drops her forehead to mine and grabs my face, looking into my eyes as we hold each other. Looking back at her, I feel an emotion rush through me that can hurt us both. Tonight everything is perfect, we're perfect, but what happens when we get back home and we have no choice but to face reality.

This woman might just have the power to break me completely . . .

Chapter Twenty-Two

Calla

IT'S THE MIDDLE OF THE night but I can't seem to sleep. I'm laying here wrapped up in Kyan's arms, wanting nothing more than to just feel him close to me. The more I lay here and watch him breathing, the more beautiful he becomes by the second.

Thinking about tomorrow and what could happen when we get home scares me. After having this feeling with Kyan, I don't think I can give it up. I had fun with Hunter. He's great, but he's not Kyan; no one is, and I don't want to be doing this with anyone else but him. I know that more now than ever.

Swallowing back my worry, I reach up and twirl a piece of his brown hair between my fingers. His grip on me tightens, pulling me even closer into his firm chest.

Savoring this moment, I press my lips to his chest while breathing in his intoxicating scent. This could quite possibly be the only moment like this that we'll get to share. That thought scares the shit out of me. After sharing the most intimate sex I've ever had in my life with this man . . . with Kyan, it might just rip my heart out to lose this, to lose him.

Pulling me up so that we're eye level, Kyan tangles our bodies together and kisses my nose. "Get some sleep, baby. No thinking. Just close your eyes."

I can't help but to notice the pain behind his voice as if he knows this is the last moment like this we'll share as well. My heart aches to hold onto this moment.

Please don't let me lose this feeling . . .

WE ARRIVED BACK AT THE apartment over an hour ago. After kissing me on the side of the mouth, like I sort of expected, Kyan took off to take care of some business at the gym. It left me feeling empty and reminded me that things are a lot more complicated than I'd hoped they would be when we returned.

I've been sitting here staring at the wall, thinking about how he made me feel yesterday when he surprised me at the wedding.

A mixture of emotions run through me, reminding me just how much of an effect this man has had over me the last few weeks. Despite me trying to shut it off, this man has been evading my every thought from the very beginning. Not even Hunter was able to push Kyan completely out of my thoughts. The problem is that Hunter might just be able to push me from Kyan's. The idea of that makes me feel sick to my stomach.

The door to the apartment opens to Tori dropping her keys down onto the table. Closing the door, she grins and runs across the room, jumping over the arm of her chair. "So . . ." Sitting up straight, she tilts her head, pushing for me to put her out of her misery. "What happened? Don't leave shit out? I want it all."

Sighing, I lay back on the couch and squeeze my eyes shut. Thinking about it just exhausts me, but that still hasn't stopped me from doing it. "Last night was absolutely incredible. I won't lie. We spent the night alternating between having rough, wild sex to having the most passionate sex of my damn life. He's so good, Tori; so damn good that it hurts to not be able to be like that now. I don't know what I'm going to do." I let out a breath and run my hands over my face in frustration.

"Wild, passionate sex sounds like a damn good time to me, so why do you look so . . . so . . . sad or some shit? I'd be all up that sexy man's ass right now instead of on this lame couch."

"Because we're back home," I huff. "Back in Chicago."

"And? What's the problem?"

I sit up enough so that I can look at her. "The problem is that what happened in Wisconsin was temporary. That's what. Back here in Chicago, we have unattached sex, personal training sessions, and his . . . brother. That's the problem."

Tori scrunches her face, finally understanding what I'm getting at. "Oh crap, honey. I didn't think about that." Standing from the couch, she rushes into the kitchen and starts pouring us some wine. "What are you going to do about Hunter? You can't seriously have feelings for that cocky asshat."

"I don't." I sit up and grab the wine glass, holding it to my lips as I think. There's only one thing I can do and the thought of it doesn't bother me one bit. "Stop having sex with Hunter, thank him for the good time, and then move on." I take a sip and set the glass down. This is the part that bothers me, the hard part. "And tell Kyan how I feel. I don't know if I can just have a sexual relationship with him anymore. I need more, Tori. With him . . . I need it all. I have to tell him before I let this go on too long and get hurt. I don't think I can handle that."

Tori takes a sip of her wine before pulling it away and running her fingers over the rim of the glass. "I would give Kyan a few days to really let his feelings set in first and then talk to him and tell him how you feel. If he can't do the whole *relationship* thing . . . then I guess you'll have to decide if you can have any kind of relationship at all. If you can't then there will be others. There will always be others."

The problem with her words is that I don't want others. I want Kyan and there's a huge chance that might not happen. She's right though. I'll give him a few days and then I'm telling him how I truly feel. He'll either feel the same way or I'll get left out in the cold and go back to *Fluffin' my own muffin.*

I just hope he'll end up being the one fluffin' it . . .

Chapter Twenty-Three

Kyan

I STARE AT MY PHONE, swallowing the thick lump in my throat. It's been three days since I dropped Calla off at her door and I haven't stopped thinking about her since. It's fucking eating at me not being next to her. Touching her and kissing her has given me a peace that I haven't felt in years. I'm missing that feeling and I want nothing more than to have it back, but the more I think about her and the way she makes me feel . . . the more I think about my brother having her in the same way that I have. He's been between those beautiful legs of hers, sucking, licking and tasting just as I have.

Whenever I close my eyes images of him fucking her torment me, driving me mad; him holding her legs open, thrusting between them, and making her scream as she comes. I fucking hate it. It makes me hate myself, because it's my fault that it happened in the first place. I was too much of a pussy to allow myself to take her completely, because I knew there was a huge chance of me falling.

"What the fuck." Tossing my phone aside, I grip my hair and hang my head between my legs. Hunter was supposed to be the solution not the fucking problem.

I should be able to give her everything she deserves. I

should be able to sleep next to her every night, holding her and making her feel beautiful. The hardest part is that I know she wants it just as badly as I do. One look into her eyes and you can see that. I may be stupid sometimes, but I'm not blind.

Not even to my own broken heart . . .

Calla

TORI AND I ARE IN the middle of editing pictures from my sister's wedding, but all I can think about is Kyan. I told myself that I would give him time and I was hoping that he would contact me, say hi, or ask me to come to a training session . . . anything, but he hasn't. The thought kills me.

I haven't spoken to Hunter either. I figured it was better to not see him for a while. Even if it is just to let him know that we can't do *this* anymore. Whatever *this* is that we've been doing. The truth is that I won't feel right seeing Hunter before seeing Kyan again. It somehow feels so wrong now.

Tori pulls up a picture of Kyan holding my face and looking into my eyes during my sister's wedding. I hear her let out a little "awe" while placing her hand to her heart.

"This man cares for you, Calla. Look at the way he's holding you. That's not something that can be faked."

Swallowing back my emotions, I take a close look at the picture, feeling my heart swell. He looks so loving holding me, that I get a little choked up.

"Next picture," I say softly. "I need to focus on getting these done."

Tori closes out of the folder and turns to look at me. "No, you don't. What you need to focus on is letting that fine piece of man meat know how you feel. You and I both know that you won't be able to function right until you do."

I laugh, unable to help myself. "I so love your insanely, crazy ass."

Tori shrugs and pulls the folder back up. "Yeah, I know. Get out of here so I can pleasure myself to this sexy man on the screen. Ryan has nothing on Kyan." She winks and I pinch her. "Ouch." She grabs her arm. "Now go. Get. I can't take you anymore until you talk to him."

Taking a long, deep breath, I stand up and mentally prepare myself. I'm not sure I can ever really be prepared for this conversation, but it has to be done. It's killing me not to know. I need to know if he has feelings for me. Even just a little bit, will be better than none.

"Crap! Here goes nothing."

Please don't break my heart . . .

Chapter Twenty-Four

Kyan

I'M JUST WRAPPING THE TOWEL around my waist when someone starts knocking at the door. It's got to be at least past ten, so automatically I expect it to be Hunter at the door.

"Dammit, Hunter." Pulling the towel tighter around my waist, I unlock the door and walk away, expecting him to shove it open and barge in. He doesn't. His ass must be sick or some shit.

I pull the door open and walk away without bothering to look behind me. Part of me wishes that I didn't even bother unlocking the door in the first place. Seeing him does nothing but stir emotions in me that I don't like.

"What the hell do you want?" I ask, while walking to the kitchen and opening the fridge.

I hear the door lightly shut before I hear the voice of the woman that has been haunting me day and night—Calla.

"Sorry. I should have called first," she says softly, her voice laced with pain.

Shit. The last thing I want to do is hurt her. I hate knowing that pain in her voice came from me.

Turning around, I quickly walk over to her and rub my thumb over her pouty bottom lip. I stare at it a few seconds too long, imagining me pulling it between my lips and sucking it. "I thought you were Hunter," I say gently. "I would never talk to you that way, Calla."

Her eyebrows pull together and I see the slight tremble of her bottom lip as she takes me in, taking time to remember every single feature as if she won't be seeing me again. "I can't do this, Kyan. I can't do this anymore."

She turns away from my touch, pushing my hand away from her face. Taking a few steps back, she sucks in a deep breath, before mumbling something under her breath.

Seeing her walking away from me only makes me want to come to her. Her pushing me away just now fucking killed me. "Can't do what? Talk to me." My jaw clenches as I stop in front of her and touch her again. I don't want her ever backing away from my touch. It stings like a bitch. "I hate you backing away from me. Don't do it, Calla."

Her eyes turn up to meet mine and my heart sinks. She looks so damn tortured that all I want to do is pull her into my bedroom and comfort her. I want to keep her there until she knows how much I care. I'm fighting so damn hard not to do that.

"With you," she breathes. "I can't pretend that I don't want more with us when the opposite is true. I want to be with you and I can't deny it anymore. I've tried so damn hard. Trust me. I know you said you didn't want anything more and I thought I could handle that, but I can't. I'm sorry."

My chest aches as I realize what she's saying. If I want her in my life then I need to give her all of me . . . including my heart. The one thing that I didn't want to give when this all started in the first place. I don't know if I can do that. It hurts too damn much to think of her with Hunter. I fucked that up. I let that happen and now we're both paying for it.

"Calla . . ." I let out a small breath and flex my jaw. I don't want to do this. I don't want to fucking hurt her. "I can't." I pull her face up, making her look me in the eyes. "Every time I fucking close my eyes I see you . . . I see you with myself and then I see you with Hunter. Every time I picture you with Hunter it makes me want to rip his throat out. My own fucking brother, Calla." I shake my head, pushing my thoughts aside. "I'm sorry."

Her eyes bounce back and forth between mine, watering as she allows my words to sink in. I see the smallest hint of a tear about to fall and it rips my heart out. "Then I should go." She pulls my hands away from her face. "I need to go. I'm sorry. I'm so sorry I came here. I didn't mean to complicate things, but I can't do this with you anymore. I'll cancel my personal training and . . ." She reaches for the handle. "I'll keep my distance when I see you."

Opening the door as she gets ready to walk out, I grip her arm, pulling her back. I can't let her walk out that fucking door without kissing her. I just need to feel her lips one last time.

Slamming her against my wall, I slam my lips to hers and kiss her harder and deeper than I've *ever* kissed anyone in my life. With each caress of our lips, my heart aches more and more.

Coming to her senses, Calla places her hands to my chest and pushes me away, turning her head away from my reach. "Don't . . ." She fights to catch her breath, her eyes heated. "Do that again. Goodbye, Kyan."

I stand here, hands in my hair as I watch her walk out my door and out my life. With the slam of my door anger bursts through me that makes me want to break everything in sight.

The worst part is that I know I only have myself to blame. I'm a stupid fucking dick and now because of that I've hurt the one person that I can't stop thinking about.

I punch the wall and growl out at the thought of her possibly being with Hunter now. There's nothing standing in her way. She could be at his door right now and he could be opening it and taking her to his bed to console her by fucking her. The thought makes me feel sick.

I stand here with my hands against the wall, just staring for the longest time. It takes me repeatedly reminding myself that this is it, for it to really begin to sink in.

Finally pulling my shit together, I reach in the fridge for my twelve pack and carry it into the bedroom, before tossing my towel aside and drinking my ass into a sleep induced coma.

So much for no one fucking getting hurt . . .

Chapter Twenty-Five

Calla

I'M TOTALLY LOST IN MY head, not even noticing the fact that Tori has been calling my name for the last five minutes. Her voice can get pretty annoying so I usually block it out anyways, but I must *really* be blocking it out right now. I finally snap out of it when she yells in my ear, causing me to jump and almost drop my damn camera.

"Tori! What the hell? Don't do that to me. I was thinking," I grind out. "Jeez."

"Exactly." She lets out an annoyed huff and walks around me to snap a few pictures of the bride and groom dancing. Apparently I've been doing a crappy job and have been kneeling here just staring like a moron. "All you've been doing for the last two days is thinking. Get out of your head before it drives you insane. Ever since you broke it off with Kyan or whatever, you're barely even here. You need to snap out of it, honey. Don't let this bring you down and ruin your career. My clicker finger hurts like hell. Now help. Snap. Snap."

Shaking my thoughts off, I focus my attention on the happy couple lovingly dancing and practically groping each other for the whole world to see. It causes an ache in my chest, reminding me just how alone I have truly been for the last two years. I've been playing it off pretty well, acting as if it hasn't affected me and that I haven't wanted *love* again, but the loss of Kyan is making it crystal clear how much I really do. The last thing I need is a slew of happy couples rubbing it in my face that I'm completely miserable. This sucks.

I barely make it through the next hour without throwing my camera at the overly happy bride's head. That sounds so bad, but she's smiling way too much for my liking right now. Every time she smiles at me I get this feeling that she knows everything and is rubbing it in my face that I suck ass and will never have what she has. Really it's just me being a miserable asshole, but oh well.

I have so much going on in my head that it's making it hard to focus on everything else at the moment. The last two days have been a complete struggle and it's actually been Tori yelling at me to get my ass in gear instead of the other way around. Talk about strange.

Another thing is that I haven't even seen Hunter to tell him how I've completely fallen on my ass for his brother that doesn't even want me back. I'm hoping that he'll understand and not take it personal. He's a good guy, but we both knew what it was to begin with. It was bound to come to an end at some point anyway. It was supposed to be the same with Kyan, yet I let myself fall like an idiot.

Hunter has texted me a few times over the last couple days, but I've lied and said I was busy. He texted me again this morning, so deciding that it's best to get it over with, I replied back asking him to meet me downstairs at the bar around nine. I know by the time I get home tonight I'm going to be too tired to meet him anywhere outside of the apartment building, and the last place I want to invite him is to my apartment. That's definitely a bad idea. I don't want to give off the wrong impression.

Happily saying goodbye to the newlyweds, Tori and I pack our equipment before stopping for some fast food and heading home. The whole time I'm eating, I'm racking my brain of the best way to explain this all to Hunter.

It's not that I'm worried it will break his heart, because I know he doesn't have feelings for me, but it's just an awkward conversation to have to begin with. This is all new to me; very new and I'm hoping it will be the last time I have to do this.

TAKING A SEAT AT THE bar, I smile when Dane makes his way over, holding a pretty blue drink in his hand. It's the same one I ordered the night I met Kyan. He's good. I like Dane.

He smiles at me and sets it down in front of me. "Feeling a little adventurous tonight?"

Laughing, I reach out for the drink and tug on the straw, splashing it around in the glass. Seeing Dane feels good right now. He's just so easy to talk to and be around. Nothing about him is complicated. I need that for a few minutes. "Thanks, Dane. You might want to keep these coming tonight. I have a feeling that it's going to be a long night. A really long night."

Throwing his towel over his shoulder, he leans against the bar and prepares to listen as if he has all night. "Trouble with the Wilder boys?" He lifts a brow and smirks when I give him a surprised look. "What? You don't think that I've seen you around here with both of them? I have eyes you know."

I clear my throat and place my straw to my lips, taking a long drink. *Mmm . . . this is so delicious. Too bad I discovered that it's not as adventurous as I had originally hoped.* Scrunching up my face, I look up at Dane and smile awkwardly. "This is awkward." I clear my throat again and laugh nervously. "It's a long story. Sort of . . . complicated . . . and twisted. It was all just meant to be for fun. I promise that they both knew. I would never . . ."

"I know," he interrupts. "You don't have to explain to me how the Wilder brothers work. Kyan has his head stuck in his career and Hunter has his head stuck in partying. I haven't known of either one of them to make a commitment. Those two sleeping with the same girl was bound to happen at some point. Don't feel stupid. I've seen other women try and fail to be in your position. You'd be surprised at how many girls practically beg to be with both Wilder men."

I tilt my head, suddenly feeling a bit of pride. *Is that weird? Hell . . . this is all weird. Does it even matter now?* "They have?" Seriously? I never would've slept with Hunter had I known. It's not something I seek. You know?"

Dane lets out an amused laugh. "I figured that about you. I've seen other girls attempt many times. They usually end up in Hunter's bed first and then attempt to hook up with Kyan. Kyan always turns them away, but I see something different when Kyan is with you. I noticed it the first night I met you. It's not the same with you, Calla. He's different. That's a huge step for him."

My heart skips a beat from his words and I find myself smiling. Knowing that Kyan looks at me differently than other girls definitely sparks a little excitement in me. The problem is . . . he doesn't look at me differently enough. Not enough for us to be together. "Yeah well . . ." I let out a small breath, feeling the ache take over again. "Kyan walked away from me. I told him how I felt and he didn't want it. I fell for him, Dane. I fell for him like an idiot and now he can't even be with me. I messed up by getting twisted up in this Wilder mess." I shake my head and sip on my straw. "I'm here to tell Hunter that we have to stop what we've been doing. I'm done with the Wilder brothers now. I have to be."

He gives me a small amused smile. "Here comes the younger one now. I hope you're ready." He grabs a beer and sets it on the bar, in front of the stool next to mine. "I'll be around if you need me." He nods behind me, saying hello to Hunter, and then turns and walks away to check on people's drinks.

I stiffen when I feel Hunter's hand wrap around my waist from behind. He quickly presses his lips to my neck before pulling away and taking a seat next to me. "Shit, you smell so damn good." He smiles and reaches for his beer, sticking his thumb in the neck of the bottle. Lifting a brow he says, "I have a feeling you have something on your mind. What's up?"

I look at him for a minute, remembering the high school Hunter and how all I wanted was to have a chance with him. It's so weird that I got that chance and now it might be the one reason that I won't get the person that I truly want to be with. It's crazy how that works.

Pulling my eyes away, I take a deep breath and just let it out. The sooner I get this over with, the sooner I can start my process of forgetting the Wilder brothers and moving on. "I feel like an idiot for saying this. I feel like an idiot for being in this situation to begin with, honestly. I never planned to just have . . . *sex;* especially with two guys, let alone two brothers. I can't do what we've been doing anymore, Hunter. I need to stop just doing this for fun." I look up to meet his eyes and he doesn't seem surprised. Not one bit. It's as if he saw it coming.

He lets out a small laugh. "Because of my brother?" He tilts back his beer, taking a quick drink. "I know, Calla. I could feel it the last time we were together. You were there, but not really. Your head was back at the gym with Kyan. You care about

Kyan. I'm not surprised. He's a good guy. He deserves for you to care about him."

"Yeah." I say relieved. "He's an amazing guy. Not that you aren't . . ."

"I'm not too bad," he says with a smile. "I'm definitely no Kyan though, right?"

"I'm sorry. It's not . . ."

"I'm kidding." He winks and pushes my leg, before gripping my knee and scooting closer to me. "You're amazing and beautiful, Calla. You're a good girl and I didn't expect what we had to go past just one night of having fun. It's just that I wanted to have sex with you so bad and for so long. I expected it to be once, but then it was so damn good that I let it keep going. It's okay. No hard feelings." He stops and brings my chin up, looking me in the eyes. "And Kyan? Have you told him how you feel? We haven't talked much lately. He's been shutting me out."

I swallow back the hurt that rises in my chest at the thought of him walking away from both of us. I don't want him to shut Hunter out and I hate him shutting me out too. That last kiss has been taunting me for days, reminding me of what I could have had. "Yeah." I grab my glass and take a long, needed drink. "He doesn't want to be with me. It's not going to work out. It's fine though. I'll be fine. I told him that we had to be more or we had to stop talking. I did my part and he wanted none of it."

He glances over my shoulder before grabbing my face and pressing his lips to mine, completely catching me off guard. Stiffening up, I try to push him away, but he only kisses me harder, making a show of it.

I push him again, finally separating our lips. "Hunter! What the hell . . ."

Out of nowhere, Kyan storms over like a maniac, slamming

Hunter against the bar. Gripping his neck, he carefully pushes me backwards and closes the distance between them.

I throw my hand over my mouth in shock and jump off of my stool as Kyan starts to go off on Hunter.

"What the fuck? Don't you ever fucking touch her like that again, asshole!" He slams him into the bar again, but harder this time, before releasing him and allowing Hunter to get back to his feet. "Stay the fuck away from her. You don't give a shit about her and you know it."

Hunter walks forward, getting in his face. "Why?" He walks into him so that their chests are touching. Both of them stand tall, neither backing down. "Does it bother you seeing her with someone else? Did it piss you off seeing my lips on hers? Huh?" Kyan pushes him backwards, but Hunter steps back in his face again. "Does it *hurt* thinking of her being with someone else?"

"It's none of your fucking business, Hunter." He gives him another shove toward the bar, causing everyone in the room to stare. "Just leave her alone before I fuck you up." Kyan presses his finger into Hunter's chest, shoving him backwards. "Is that why you called me down here, asshole?"

Hunter pushes Kyan's hand away and shakes his head. "No, *brother.* I called you down here so I could open your fucking eyes. You've fallen for her, but you've been so set on keeping your heart closed off that you've been fighting it like a moron." He gets in Kyan's face, causing Kyan to steel his jaw as he listens to what Hunter has to say. "You needed to see that Calla doesn't want me. Not like she wants you. That's why I called you down here. So open your fucking eyes before it's too late. I'm tired of seeing you alone and miserable. Fuck! It's been three years now."

Hunter turns away and slams back his beer, breathing hard

in between gulps.

Kyan runs his hands through his hair, breathing heavily, until his eyes land on me. His breathing slowly evens out and his eyes fill with pain, as he looks me over from head to toe like he hasn't seen me in months.

I want nothing more than to run into his arms and hold him, but I don't. I know that I don't have the right to do that, but I want it more than anything.

Looking at Hunter, Kyan grabs his beer out of his hand and tilts it back, looking him in the face. Then he slams the empty bottle down onto the bar. "I know," he says.

"What?" Hunters asks, looking his brother over.

"That I fell for Calla." He turns to me and grabs my face, looking me in the eyes. "I can't fucking stop thinking about you. I've tried so damn hard, but it's impossible." He brushes his lips against mine before tangling his hands into the back of my hair and gently kissing me.

Grabbing his arms, I kiss him back, smiling against his lips. My heart is racing so damn fast that it's hard to catch my breath. His lips give me that familiar feeling of peace that I've been missing since the wedding. I have completely fallen for this man and this kiss confirms that he's fallen for me too; at least I hope.

Pulling away from me, he rubs his thumb over my bottom lip while sucking his lip into his mouth. "I just needed some time to think and figure out shit in my head. The more I thought about it, the more I realized that it was too late. I've already given you my damn heart and I don't want it back." He leans down and smiles against my lips. "I want you," he whispers.

"Thank fucking God." Hunter grunts from beside us. "I'm going home."

Stopping Hunter, Kyan reaches for his arm. "We're not

done yet, asshole. We have a lot of shit to talk about later. Alright, little brother?"

Hunter grins before leaning in to attempt to kiss my forehead. Kyan places his hand over his face, pushing him back. "No way. Your lips won't be going anywhere near Calla for a while. A *long* while."

A small laugh escapes me as I watch the brothers making up. They don't need to say it aloud I can see it in their eyes. They may have their problems, but they love each other. It makes me want to go home and call Chrissy. It makes me miss her like crazy and want what they have.

Kyan apologizes to Dane and everyone, before turning back to me and pulling me against him. Swallowing, he pulls my chin up to look at him. "I'm sorry for being an idiot. If you give me a chance, I will make it up to you."

Smiling, I bite his bottom lip and pull away. "You definitely have a lot of making up to do, Kyan Wilder." I wrap my arms around him and press my face to his chest as he pulls me against him as closely as he can.

Being in his arms feels so insanely good that I really don't want to think about the past or the future. All that matters is the present. I want this man and he wants me. That's all I can ask for.

The sexy guy with a gym bag and firm ass . . . I never expected he'd be mine.

Chapter Twenty-Six

Calla

One month later . . .

OPENING KYAN'S DOOR, I let myself in and throw my purse down onto the kitchen island. Kyan asked me to throw on something fun and meet him here after the wedding. He sounded pretty excited on the phone, which only got me extremely excited.

"Kyan . . . get your sexy ass out here." I shout. "I need to touch you before I go crazy."

Kyan walks out of the bathroom rolling the sleeves to his black button down up to his elbows. Smirking, he walks over and grabs my hands, rubbing them over his chest. "Mmm . . ." He leans down and kisses me roughly on the lips, as if he's been dying to kiss me all day. "You look damn sexy in that dress, baby." He pulls my hands away from his chest and bites his bottom lip. "I can't let you touch me too much right now or I'm going to end up fucking you all night instead of going out."

He walks into the living room and bends down to pick up something from the table.

A huge smile takes over my face as soon as I realize what it is. I have been waiting for what seems like forever to hold this in my hands. I hurry over to him and snatch it out of his hands.

"The book!" I shriek. My eyes widen as I look it over, flipping it back and forth, checking out my pictures on the cover. "It's so beautiful. Wow. This is so cool, Kyan. I'm starting this book tonight. We might just have to hold off sex until I'm done."

He snatches the book out of my hand and playfully starts kissing my neck, causing me to scream and laugh at the same time. "Stop it! Kyan . . ." I push at his chest as he continues to make me squirm. "That tickles. That tickles, stop."

Finally, he stops and pulls my body against him. He wraps his hand into the back of my hair and looks me in the eyes. "I don't think I can ever go a day without being inside you, Calla. You know that." He raises a brow and motions with his head toward the book. "I will make love to you while you read it if I have to. Just imagine my extremely hard cock inside of you, pushing in and out while you read about this *Blaine* guy. I'll be sure to remind you that the real thing is so much better. Don't test me."

I laugh and smile against his lips. I rub my thumb over his bottom lip just like he always does to me. "I'm going to hold you to that." Reaching up, I kiss him gently before pulling away and getting ready to walk toward the door.

I feel a pull on my arm, stopping me. Kyan slowly moves to stand in front of me. His eyes look deep into mine as if he's looking into my soul, burning himself into it, and ensuring that it will never forget him. "I love you, Calla." He swallows. "I have for a while now. So fucking much."

My heart literally skips a beat and the butterflies in my stomach go crazy as I realize what he just said. I've been long-ing to hear those words for what seems like a lifetime. I was seriously starting to go insane waiting.

Wrapping my arms around his neck, I pull him down to me and slam my lips against his. I kiss him so hard that it hurts my lips, but I don't care. My emotions are going crazy and I don't care if he sees. I want him to feel how much I have waited for these three little words.

"I love you, Kyan. I love you *so* much that it hurts in your absence."

He rubs his thumbs over my face and smiles. "Nothing will never have to hurt with me, baby. I promise that." He kisses me one more time, gently caressing my face, before grabbing my hand. "Let's get downstairs so we can hurry back up to bed." He smirks and bounces his eyebrows, being sure that I get what he means, as if it's never clear with him.

This man is absolutely perfect and I love it. This is perfect . . .

WHEN WE GET DOWNSTAIRS TORI and Hunter start whistling and calling us over to a table in the back, as if we can't see their crazy asses. They pushed two long tables together to make room for all seven of us: Kyan, Tori, Hunter, Dane, his beautiful wife, Olivia, and me.

I've met Olivia once before at the gym and she's the sweetest little thing that you'll ever meet. She's just a little over five feet with long, black hair and big, kind, blue eyes. She's so damn cute. I adore her already.

Tori immediately jumps to her feet and runs over to me, grabbing my arm. "Oh thank God you're here. I don't know how much longer I can look at Hunter without wanting to staple his mouth shut." She makes a face over her shoulder in Hunter's direction. "He's so hot, but his mouth seriously needs some work."

I roll my eyes and laugh as Hunter raises his drink and

smirks. "My mouth can definitely work on you," he teases. "It can work a lot of things."

Tori reaches over to the table and throws a fry at his head. "You drive me crazy. I love food. I *fucking* love it, which means that I eat it, not throw it. Get what I mean, moron?"

I laugh against Tori's shoulder as Hunter just shrugs, picks up the fry, and eats it before turning to talk to Dane and his wife.

Seeing Dane here makes me so happy. Kyan forced fewer hours on Dane and doubled his pay. Dane argued it at first, but is definitely enjoying his time off from work now. Based on what Kylie says, he takes her out once a week for a romantic night with just the two of them. It doesn't surprise me. Dane seems like the hopeless romantic. They got married a couple weeks ago and Tori and I had the honor of photographing it. I actually shed a few tears. I won't lie.

Kyan comes up behind me and wraps his arms around my waist, pulling me into him as him and Olivia chat over her next cover and how she wants me to photograph Kyan again. I'm so happy I can seriously scream right now. I have been waiting for her to ask for what feels like *forever.*

"I'll do it!" I scream, scaring everyone at the table. I shrug and pop a fry into my mouth. "What? I can't contain my excitement. You know that." I lean my head against Kyan's chest, completely satisfied, and smile as everyone goes back to their previous activities.

Watching Hunter get under Tori's skin from across the table only makes the high that much better. She needs someone to annoy her just as much as she annoys me. Brad obviously wasn't a match for her and she kicked him to the curb a few weeks ago. She's been up mine and Kyan's ass ever since, constantly asking about our sex life. I can't take it anymore. She needs to get some before I stop having sex just to shut her up.

Actually . . . I take that back. I can't do that. Not with being in Kyan's bed each night.

Olivia pulls my attention away from Tori and Hunter. Excitedly, I lean over and give her a hug, shaking her in my arms. Tonight is her night. This is about her and her book, and Kyan was so amazing to set this gathering up for her.

Releasing Olivia, she throws her hand over her mouth in excitement as Mya, one of the other bartenders, comes over and sets a small cake down on the table with Olivia's book on it.

"Oh my goodness. I'm going to cry," Olivia says behind her hand. "Thank you!"

She turns to Kyan and pulls him in for a hug, while pulling me in at the same time.

"It was all Calla," Kyan says, while squeezing us.

"What?" I ask in surprise. "I didn't even know the book was released." I push his arm as he releases us. "You big softy. Awe." Everyone else says awe at the same time, causing Kyan to roll his eyes and smile, while grabbing for his beer.

"Yeah. Yeah. Just eat up," he groans.

I throw my arms back around him and mouth that I love him and he does the same in return before kissing me gently on the lips.

Things seriously couldn't be any better than they are right this minute. I'm with my friends, the people most important to me, my sister is coming to stay next weekend, and I'm in the arms of the man I love.

I'm completely whole right now and I plan on holding onto this feeling for as long as I can . . .

The End

Read on for an excerpt of SLADE

WALK OF SHAME #1

VICTORIA ASHLEY

CHAPTER ONE
Slade

It's dark.

I love it with the lights off. She insisted on teasing me this way. My arms are tied behind me, my naked body bound to a chair. Goose bumps prickle my flesh as she softly blows on my hard cock, almost breaking my willpower. Her lips are so close, yet not close enough. I insist on teasing *her* this way.

"Na ah, not yet, baby."

She tilts her head up, her blond hair cascading over her shoulders as her eyes lock with mine. They're intense, desperate. She's silently begging me with her eyes, asking me to let her touch me already. I'm used to this. She needs to learn that when you're in my house we play by my rules. "Slade," she whimpers. "Come on already."

"Look down, baby." She tilts her head back down and runs her tongue over her lips as she eagerly looks at my cock; no doubt imagining what it tastes like in her mouth. "That's it. Don't move."

I lift my hips, bringing the tip of my head to brush her lips. "You want me in your mouth?"

She nods her head and lets out a sound between a moan

and a growl. Damn, it's such a turn on.

"How bad do you want it? I want to fucking hear it?"

Her nails dig into my thighs as she growls in aggravation. "More than anything. I want it so just give it to me, dammit. You already know how bad I want it."

A deep laugh rumbles in my throat as she scratches her nails down my legs in an attempt to hurt me. What she doesn't realize is that I welcome the pain. I get off on it.

"Is that all you got, pussycat?" I tease. "If you want my cock, you're going to have to do better than that."

She looks angry now; determined. Standing up, she points a finger in my chest. "You're the one tied up. This is supposed to be my game. Why do *you* have to torture me and make me wait?"

Biting my bottom lip, I nod for her to move closer to me. When she gets close to my face, I slide my tongue out and run it over her lips, causing her to tremble as I taste her. "Show. Me. How. Much. You. Want. Me."

Straddling me, she screams and slaps me hard across the face before yanking my head back by my hair. If I could get any harder, I would.

Fuck me.

"Now, that's what I'm talking about." I press my stiff cock against her ass, showing her just how turned on I am. Then I look her in the eye. "Show me what you can do with your mouth. First impression is always the most important."

A mischievous smile spreads across her face as she slithers her way off my lap and down between my legs. Gripping my thighs in her hands, she runs her tongue over the tip of my dick before suctioning it into her mouth. It hits the back of her throat, causing her to gag. She doesn't care; completely uninhibited. She just shoves it deeper.

Fuck yeah.

I moan as she swirls her tongue around my shaft while sucking at the same time. It feels fucking fantastic. "I told you it's worth the wait, baby. Just wait until I get inside you. It feels better than it tastes."

She pulls back and licks her lips. "Then why don't you show me. My pussy has never been so wet." She stands up and bends over in front of me, exposing her wet lips. I can see the moisture glistening from here; beckoning to suck me inside. She smiles as she runs her fingers over the folds as if she's teasing me; testing me. "You like that?" she asks seductively, tantalizing me. "You want this tight little pussy all for yourself, you greedy little bastard?"

I nod, playing into her little game. She seems to think she's in charge.

"Well, come and get it." She inserts her fingers into her mouth and sucks them clean, before shoving them into her entrance, fucking me with her eyes. Her ass moves up and down in perfect rhythm as she purrs. "I'm waiting." She shoves her fingers deeper. "I want to see those muscles flexing as you ram into me. I want you to . . ."

Well you won't be waiting for long.

Breaking free from my restraints, I stand up, grab her hips and flip her around before slamming her back up against the wall. "What were you saying, baby?" I growl into her ear. I grip both of her ass cheeks and lift her as she wraps her legs around my waist, squeezing. "I'm not sure you can handle what I have to offer." I grip her face in my hand before leaning in and biting her bottom lip, roughly tugging. "You're finally about to get what you've wanted. I just hope you don't have shit to do for the next few days because this might get a little rough. Last time to make your escape, because once I start there's no stopping until you're screaming my name loud; so loud it fucking hurts my ears." I search her eyes waiting to see if she's changed her mind; nothing but raw heat and lust. She still wants it. She's brave. No girl walks into my bed and walks out unscathed. So, she'll get it. I lift an eyebrow. "Okay, then."

I take wide strides across the room to my king-sized bed and toss her atop the mattress. Before she can blink, I am between her thighs, spreading them wide for me. I run my tongue up her smooth flesh, stopping at intersection of her thighs and clean shaven pussy. "You ready for me to make you come without even touching you?"

I begin blowing my cool breath across her swollen, wet pussy. She thrusts her hips up; no doubt her hungry little pussy wanting more and just as I'm about to show her my skills, there's a knock at the damn door.

Bad fucking timing.

Gritting my teeth, I shake my head and look toward the door. "Give me a sec." I step down from the bed and motion for Lex to cover up. When she's done, I call for Cale to come in. "Okay, man."

The door opens right as I'm reaching for my pack of cigarettes and switching the light on. My dick is still standing at full alert, but I could care less. This shit head interrupted my night. If he doesn't like seeing my dick hard, then he should have known better than to come up to my room in the middle of the night.

Stepping into my room, Cale takes notice of my hard on and quickly reaches for the nearest item of clothing and tosses it on my dick. I look down to see a shirt hanging from it. I shake it off. "A little warning next time, mother fucker. I'm tired of witnessing that shit."

Lighting my cigarette, I laugh and take a drag. "Jealous, prick?"

Ignoring me, he walks past me when he sets eyes on Lex. She's been coming to the club for a while now and she's sexy as hell. All of the guys have been trying to get with her, but she's wanted nothing but my cock this whole time. He raises his eyebrows and slides onto the foot of my bed. "Damn, Lex. You get sexier every time I see you."

Gripping the sheet tighter against her body, Lex growls and kicks Cale off the bed. "Go fuck off, Cale. I don't want your dick."

Jumping up with a quickness, Cale reaches for my jeans and tosses them to me. "I don't want to fuck you, Lex. I want to pleasure you. This dick is special." He nods toward me. "Unlike Slade's."

"Fuck you, Cale. What the hell do you want?"

He turns to me after smirking at Lex. "The club just called. We gotta go."

"It's not my night to work, man. Isn't Hemy working?" I take a long drag of my cigarette, letting the harsh smoke fill my lungs as I close my eyes. I really need to release this tension. I will fuck her in front of him if I have to. It wouldn't be the first time I've fucked in front of an audience. "I'm a little busy right now." I dangle Lex's thong from my finger. "If you can't tell."

Not getting where I'm going with this, Cale pulls out his phone and starts typing something in it. "We need to go now. There's a bachelorette party and the chicks asked for us specifically. You know what that means. Plus, Hemy is getting eaten alive right now."

Oh shit. I didn't think it was possible, but my cock just got even harder.

"Well, then I guess we better get started." I put out the

cigarette, push past Cale and slide under the sheet. I reach for the condom on the nightstand and rip the wrapper open with my teeth. "This is going to have to be a quick one," I mumble before spitting the wrapper out and rolling the condom over my erection.

Lex looks at me questionably and nods to Cale. "You're going to have sex with me while he watches?"

I smirk as I flip her over and shove her head down into the mattress. "If he doesn't get out of my room, then yes, I'm going to fuck you while he watches." I peek over my shoulder at Cale and he lifts an eyebrow, his interest now peaked. "You've got three seconds and the counting started two seconds ago."

Pointing to Lex, he starts walking backwards while chewing his bottom lip. "As much as I'd love to watch you get fucked, I'm out. This dude gets too wild and I'll probably hurt myself just watching." Picking my wallet up from my dresser, he tosses it at my head, but misses. "Hurry your ass up. I'm changing my shit right now and then we need to go."

Lex moans from below me as I grip her hips, pull her to me and slide inside her. She's extra wet for me, making it easy to give her a good quick fuck. "You're so fucking wet. You were craving this cock weren't you?"

"Dude," Cale complains from a distance; although, I can still feel his eyes watching us.

"Your three seconds were up." I thrust my hips, gripping her hair in both my hands. "Mmm . . . fuck." *Damn that feels good.* "I'll be out in a minute."

"Leave, Cale!" Lex moans while gripping the sheet. "Oh shit! You feel even better than what I've been told. So thick and oh shit . . . it's so deep."

"Damn, that's hot."

"Out!" Lex screams.

"I'm out. I'm out." Cale backs his way out, shutting the door behind him. The truth is, if it weren't for Lex kicking him out, I could've cared less if he stayed and watched. I'm not ashamed.

Knowing I don't have a lot of time, I need to get this chick off fast. That's my rules and I don't have many. She gets off, then I get off. There is no stopping in between for me. Once I start, this is a done deal.

I can feel her wetness thickening. "You've gotten wetter. You like him watching, huh?" I yank her head back and run my tongue over her neck before whispering, "I would've let him stay; let him watch me as I fuck your wet pussy. Does that turn you on?"

Before she can say anything else, I push her head back down into the mattress and slam into her while rubbing my thumb over her swollen clit.

Her hands grip the sheets as she screams out and bites down on her arm, trying to silence her orgasm.

Slapping her ass, I ball my fist in her hair and gently pull it back so her back is pressed against my chest. "Don't hold it back. I want to fucking hear it. Got it?" She shakes her head so I thrust into her as deep as I can go. "Show me how it feels."

Screaming, she reaches back and grabs my hair, yanking it to the side. This makes me fuck her even harder. "Oh yes! Oh God! Slade, don't stop."

Reaching around, I grab her breast in one hand squeezing roughly and bite into her shoulder, rubbing my finger of the opposite hand faster over her slick clit. Her body starts to tremble beneath me as she clamps down hard on my cock. "Oh, shit. Stop, I can't take it. It feels so good, Slade."

I grip her hips and brush my lips over her ear. "You want me to stop?" I pull out slowly, teasing her. "You don't want this cock filling your pussy?" I shove it back in, causing her head to bang into the wall. "Huh, do you want me to stop?"

She shakes her head. "No, don't stop. Shit, don't stop!"

"That's what I thought." I push her completely flat on her stomach, holding my body weight with one arm as I grip the back of her neck and fuck her with all my strength. I want her to remember this because it's the only time she'll be getting my cock and we both know it. It's how I work.

She's squirming below me, shaking as if she's in the middle of another orgasm. "Slade! Oh shit!"

A few thrusts later and I'm ready to blow my load. Pulling out, I bite her ass and stroke my cock as I come.

The relief gives me a high; a fucking drug that I can't get enough of. Nothing else makes me feel this way. Actually, nothing else makes me feel. This is it for me.

My own personal hell.

CHAPTER TWO

Slade

CLOSING MY EYES, I TILT back my second shot of Whiskey. *That's it,* I think, moaning as it leaves a raw, burning sensation in the back of my throat. It's what I need; what I crave.

After rushing Lex out of my room and listening to Cale ramble on about one of his old friends crashing with us for the next week, I need this damn rush; the alcohol pumping through my veins, weakening my demons. Hell, I might even go for another one just for the numbness.

Fuck it. Why not.

Holding up my empty shot glass, I nod at Sarah to come my way. She instantly drops what she's doing to come to me. "Give me another one."

Snatching my empty glass away, she smiles and nods over to Cale and Hemy working their shit on the girls in the back corner. "Shouldn't you be over there showing them how it's done?" She laughs while pulling out a bottle of Jack and filling a new shot glass. "They're both looking a little tired and worn down. You know how bachelorette's are; last night of freedom and all."

I turn around in my stool and look at the two idiots. Cale is standing on a couch grinding his cock in some girl's face while wiping sweat from his forehead. Hemy has some girl on the floor, rolling his body above hers, but he's moving in a rhythm slower than the music.

Tired? How the hell can they . . .

"Yeah, well give me another shot and then I'll show them what's up."

"I'm sure you will, Slade. Keep slamming these back and I might be showing you what's up later." She pushes the shot of Whiskey across the bar and I grab it. "Go ahead. Drink up." She winks.

Smirking, I hold the glass to my lips. She already knows how I work. "We've already had our night, Sarah." I tilt the glass back and run my tongue over my lips, slowly, just to remind her of how I pleasured her. This causes her to swallow hard and her breathing to pick up. "It was hot as fuck too." I slide the glass forward and stand up. "But it goes against my rules."

Her eyes linger down to the very noticeable bulge in my jeans. She smiles while running her finger over the empty glass. "Good to know I can at least still get you hard."

I toss down a twenty and start backing away. "Baby, you get every man hard." I point to the awkward looking guy that has been staring at her since I sat at the bar. "Especially that dude."

She glances at the scrawny dude with glasses and forces a smile. He smiles back and leans over the bar, awaiting conversation. "I so hate you, Slade," she growls and I love it. Growling turns me on.

"That's all right. I'm used to it."

She tosses a straw at me and I knock it away with my hand before turning around and making my way over to the bachelorette party.

The girls are tossing back drinks; some of them standing on tables while a few of them are watching from afar. Those are usually the married ones; the good girls. That's all right though, because I don't need to touch them to pleasure them. They'll still get off.

As I'm about to show my boys up, to my right, I notice two girls dancing and minding their own business. Instantly, my focus goes to the curvy body that is swaying back and forth, drawing my cock to instant attention. It's so seductive it makes my cock hurt.

Skin tight blue jeans mold to her every curve, making me imagine what it would be like to run my tongue over that tight little ass; to taste every inch of her.

Letting my dick do the talking, I walk up to the dance floor, grab the drink out of her hand and set it down on the table beside me.

She looks pissed off, but that's all right. Pissed is sexy as hell on her. It makes me want her more. Her eyes stray from the table I just set her glass on and land on my stomach. Then my chest. Then, slowly, up to my face. She swallows and a look of lust flashes in her eyes. She wants me and I haven't even done anything yet.

Holy fuck. She is beautiful.

My eyes trail from her long blond hair that stops just below her breasts up to her red pouty lips. Damn, I want to suck those between my lips. She's looking at me through long, thick lashes and even in the dimmed lighting; I can see that she has two different colored eyes. I can't make out the colors, but I can see the shade difference.

So fucking hot.

"Umm . . ." She smiles and runs her hand through her hair.

"Can I help you with something? We kind of have a private party going on here."

Taking a step closer, I lean in and brush my lips over her ear. "Yeah, I can help you with something," I whisper. "I can help you with a lot of things."

Her breathing picks up and I already know that I have her. It's that simple. "I'm sorry, but I don't even know you." She takes a step back, but her eyes trail down my body before coming back up to meet my face. She looks nervous. I love that. I can teach her a few things. "And I was drinking that."

I watch her with a smirk as she reaches for her drink and pretends to give me a dirty glare. It's not working on me though. I already know her body language and she's already let it slip that I do something to her. "I can give you something better than that."

Her tiny nostrils flare as her eyes rake back down my body, stopping on my fucking crotch. If that's what she wants then I'll give it to her. "Sorry, but I'm not interested. I'm just here for a friend's party."

She likes games. Good thing, because I like them too.

Closing the distance between our bodies, I cup her cheek in my hand. I bring my lips close to hers while looking her in the eyes. Her breath hitches as I press my body against hers and bring my eyes down to meet her lips. "Are you sure about that?"

Her lips begin to move as if she's about to respond and I have the sudden urge to suck them into my mouth; to own them. She's breathing heavy and I can feel the heat radiating from between her thighs that are pressed against my leg while I rub my thumb over her cheekbone.

I feel myself leaning closer until my bottom lip brushes hers. "You're fucking beautiful."

She takes in a quick burst of air and takes a step back. "Umm . . ."

"Slade!" A drunken female shrieks from behind me.

Shit. I hate shriekers.

Exhaling, I turn my head, but keep my eyes glued to the beautiful blond in front of me. For some reason, I don't want to take my eyes away.

Those lips. Fuck me, I want to fuck them. I want them wrapped around my cock.

"About time you got here." A dark haired woman with huge fake tits bounces in front of me and grabs my hand, pulling me away from the beauty in front of me. I see blondie's eyes glance down at my hand, but she quickly turns her head away and clears her throat as if embarrassed. "My favorite piece of eye candy is here." She throws her arms up and starts screaming while pulling me away. "Look everyone. It's fucking, Slade," she slurs.

Smiling to blondie as she watches me, I mouth, "You're mine later."

Her lips part and I can tell she just swallowed. I have her thinking about it. It's written all over her face. Her friend starts nudging her in the side until finally she pulls her eyes away from me and smiles nervously at her friend.

Shit, I've gotta have her. I won't stop until I do.

Spinning on my heel, I pick the brunette up by her hips and sit her down on the chair in front of us. She spreads wide for me and presses her hands against my chest as I step between her legs and slowly grind my hips to the music.

Placing one hand behind my head, I grip her neck with my other as I close the space between our bodies, grinding my hips in a slow, seductive movement as if I'm slowly fucking her.

She moans from beneath me as I let her hands explore my

chest and abs. The women here like to touch and I like to give them what they want. It's my job to please them and I'm damn good at it.

"Take it off!" A few girls start screaming.

"Let us see your body. Come on!"

Absofuckinglutely.

Pulling the brunette's chin up, I look her in the eyes as I slowly pull my shirt over my head and toss it down beside me. Most women love it when I make them feel like I'm stripping just for them. It makes them feel special.

She bites her bottom lip as her hands go straight for the muscles leading down to my cock. The girls can never get enough of it; of both.

As much as I'm enjoying getting these women off, there's one woman in particular I want to get off and I'll be damned if I'm going to let her leave here unsatisfied.

CHAPTER THREE
Aspen

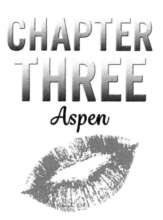

Kayla keeps nudging me to get my attention, but for some reason I can't seem to drag my eyes away from the jerk-off that is practically dry humping some girl in the corner. She loves it too; over there moaning and rubbing her hands all over his body as if she's about to have an orgasm. How gross. Have some damn class. We aren't in the middle of a damn porn.

A stripper? I shake my head and snort. *A sexy as hell one too. Who the hell does he think he is getting that close to me?*

The bad part of it is, I think he may just be the sexiest man I have ever laid eyes on. Messy black hair that falls over his deep blue eyes and the perfect five o'clock shadow that surrounds a set of full lips. I can't forget that body of pure muscle that you could easily see through that firm fitting white T-shirt he had on. Now, it's off and . . . *crap*. He has me so worked up, I can barely breathe. *This is embarrassing.*

Our lips were so close I could almost taste him. I imagine he probably tastes minty and fresh; perfectly refreshing. For some stupid reason, I had the urge to run my tongue over those full lips. They just looked so soft and inviting; calling me to feel them, suck them. The way he was looking at me; holy shit, it was like he was tasting me in a way I have never been tasted. I liked it. Dammit, why did I like it?

"Um . . . Aspen. Hello. Am I talking to my damn self? Snap out of it."

I suck in a deep breath and pull my eyes away from Mr. Sex himself. "What? I'm listening." I bring my eyes up to meet hers, but they quickly stray back over to *him* as I pretend to pay attention to her.

Brushing her burgundy locks over her shoulder, she rolls her eyes at me and grabs my hand. "Come on. Let's just get closer so you can drool over sexy stripper boy up close. There's nothing to be ashamed of. Stop being so shy. We're here to have fun."

I huff and pull my hand out of her grip. There's no way I'm going over there and giving him the pleasure of seeing me watching him. I'm only here because Paige is getting married. Hell, I'm not even watching *Cale* and I've known him for years. I'll just stay where I'm at. No thank you.

"I'm good, Kayla. I'm not getting in the middle of that orgasm fest. It's pathetic." I hold my drink up and grin. "This is all the pleasure I need while I'm here. Simple as that." I take a huge gulp as my eyes once again land on him and *oh God, that ass.*

His jeans are now hanging half way down his ass, showing his muscular butt cheeks through his white boxer briefs. The busty woman in front of him is desperately tugging on the front of his jeans, working on pulling them down his body. I don't blame her. I want to take them off with my teeth.

Crap, my mind is in the gutter.

Placing his hands behind her head, he pulls her face down by his crotch as he starts grinding his hips up and down in perfect rhythm to the song playing. It's a slow, seductive song that makes me think about sex. Yup, I'm definitely thinking about sex now.

Just as I think he's about to actually let this woman publicly suck his dick or something, he grips her by the hips and pulls her up to her feet. Slowly, he makes his way behind her and his eyes land on me and they stay there, locked with mine.

What the . . . why? Stop looking at me.

I tug on the collar of my white blouse and without meaning to I start fanning myself off. He smiles at this, knowing exactly what he's doing to me. He's doing this on purpose.

Cocky jerk.

Bending the girl over, he grips her hair in one hand and pulls her neck back while grinding his hips on her ass. His eyes bore into mine as he shakes himself out of his jeans and lets all of his sexiness consume us. Yes, he is damn sexy and he knows it. That just pisses me off more. His legs are thick and muscular; covered with random tattoos and every muscle in his body is well sculpted.

Now that he's facing me it's easy to see his defined chest and abs flexing as he moves with the music. The muscles leading down to his briefs are staring at me, flexing with each sway of his hips; calling out to be touched and licked. *Mmm yes. I want a taste . . .*

Holy hell, he's in shape; like a fitness model. Plus, he has random tattoos inked across his chest, sides, lower stomach and arms as well. Hell, he has tattoos all over and it makes him even hotter. They glisten as the perspiration forms on his skin.

He's staring at me, while practically having sex with this girl with his clothes on. Still, I'm standing here watching as if it were me.

What is wrong with me?

I feel myself start to sweat and get a tingling sensation

between my thighs as he bites his bottom lip and starts thrusting hard and deep while his eyes devour me. Well, at least I imagine it would be really deep. I can't deny that I bet it would feel so good.

He must notice me sweating because he laughs a little and steps away from the girl that is still bent over with her ass in the air. Ignoring all the girls screaming for him, he starts walking with meaning; unstoppable. With each step, he gets closer and closer to me.

My body is shaking just from his presence and my breathing picks up. I hate my body right now.

His eyes are intense; telling me he wants me as his. A part of me almost wants to give in just from that look alone.

My eyes slowly leave his eyes, searching my way down his muscular body and landing right on his hard dick.

Oh. My. God.

You can see everything through his tight briefs. The thickness of his dick and even the shape of its head. The whole package. He's so . . . hard.

Stopping in front of me, he smirks and tilts his head down toward his cock. My eyes are betraying me. *Damn bastards.* They won't move away. "You know, it's against the rules, but I would let you touch it if you wanted to."

Shaking my head, I pull my eyes away and slam back the rest of my drink. This is my third one and I'm a lightweight; probably not a good thing. I take a step back as he takes a step closer. Clearing my throat, I ask, "Touch what?"

Reaching out, he grabs my hand and places it on the V of muscles that lead down to his briefs, slowly sliding it down his sweaty, slick body. "My cock," he whispers.

My body clenches from his words and I hate it. Yanking my hand away, I grab Kayla by the arm and slam my empty glass down onto the table beside me. I need to get out of here. "Thanks for the offer, playboy, but I'm here to meet a friend and like I said, I'm not interested."

Smirking, he takes a step back as Cale slaps him on the shoulder. "Dude, back away from our temporary roommate. You're freaking Aspen the fuck out, Sir Dick a lot."

I see the smile in his eyes as if he's got me right where he wants me now and he looks like a man that always gets what he wants. Running his tongue over his bottom lip, he backs away slowly, keeping his eyes on me the whole time, until disappearing back into his crowd of fan girls.

Cale gives me a quick hug and apologizes. "Sorry about him. Just ignore him and you'll be fine." He starts backing away and smiles. "We'll catch up later, I promise."

"All right, pretty boy," I call out. "Better hurry and get back to your crazy fan girls."

Cale is the definition of pretty. Short blond hair, striking green eyes and the sweetest dimpled smile you'll ever see. I will never understand why my sister has never hooked up with him.

Turning to Kayla, I let out a deep breath and instantly turn red with embarrassment as she starts laughing. "What!" I yell.

She smirks and pretends like she's giving a blowjob.

"Stop that! You dirty, bitch." I push her shoulder and she laughs. "I need another drink."

She turns toward Slade, dancing his dick off in the middle of some girls. "I would need a drink after that too. Holy shit! That is one fine piece of ass." She starts pulling me towards the bar. "Plus, you need to get your mind off a certain someone," she says to remind me. "Relax a little."

"Yeah," I breathe. "Probably so. I'm not going to let it bring me down this week."

When we reach the bar, the pretty bartender smiles at me and shakes her head.

Wondering if she's laughing at me for some reason, I take a seat on the stool in front of me and give her a hard look. Slade has me all kinds of feisty at the moment and I can't believe he's Cale's roommate. Not good. "What?" I narrow my eyes at her as she reaches for an empty glass.

Scooping up some ice, she looks over my shoulder and laughs again. "Honey, no one turns Slade down. Are you insane? That is one piece of ass that you don't want to miss out on. Trust me."

Trying my best not to look behind me, I fail. I should kick my own ass. I glance over my shoulder to see Slade staring at me while using his shirt to wipe the sweat off his chest. He slowly moves it down his body as if teasing me.

Crap! He even looks sexy doing that.

I growl under my breath and ignore what she just said. Obviously, he's a man whore. "Just give me another drink, please. Make it strong."

The bartender tilts her head and goes about her business. Thank goodness because I really don't want to think about that half naked, sexy asshole anymore.

"Right on," Kayla says happily. "It's a good thing I'm driving your ass around."

"Probably a very good thing right now," I say softly, trying to get my thoughts in check.

After setting eyes on the sexiest asshole I have ever seen, I have a feeling I'm going to need help if I'm going to be in the same house with *him* for the next week.

Crap, I'm in for a ride.

Discover Slade and the rest of the
Walk of Shame Series, Available Now

Acknowledgments

FIRST AND FOREMOST, I'D LIKE to say a big thank you to all my loyal readers that have given me support over the last couple years and have encouraged me to continue with my writing. Your words have all inspired me to do what I enjoy and love. Each and every one of you mean a lot to me and I wouldn't be where I am if it weren't for your support and kind words.

I'd also like to thank my special friend, Author of the Fate Series and editor, Charisse Spiers. She has put a lot of time into helping me put this story together. I'm lucky to have her be a part of this journey with me. Please everyone look out for her books. She has shown me so much support through this whole process and it would be nice to be able to return the favor. Her stories are beautifully written and something that the world shouldn't miss out on.

My amazingly, wonderful PA, Amy Preston Rogers. She helped me from the very beginning of Thrust when it was just a thought in my head. Her support has meant so much to me.

Also, all of my beta readers, both family and friends that have taken the time to read my book and give me pointers throughout this process. You guys have helped encourage me more than you know. *Bestsellers and Beststellars of Romance* for hosting my cover reveal, blog tour and release day blitz. Hetty Whitmore Rasmussen has been a big part in making this happen. You all have. Thank you all so much.

I'd like to thank another friend of mine, Clarise Tan from *CT Cover Creations* for creating my cover. You've been wonderful to work with and have helped me in so many ways.

Thank you to my boyfriend, friends and family for understanding my busy schedule and being there to support me through the hardest part. I know it's hard on everyone, and everyone's support means the world to me.

Last but not least, I'd like to thank all of the wonderful book bloggers that have taken the time to support my book and help spread the word. You all do so much for us authors and it is greatly appreciated. I have met so many friends on the way and you guys are never forgotten. You guys rock. Thank you!

About the Author

VICTORIA ASHLEY GREW UP IN Rockford, IL and has had a passion for reading for as long as she can remember. After finding a reading app where it allowed readers to upload their own stories, she gave it a shot and writing became her passion.

She lives for a good romance book with tattooed bad boys that are just highly misunderstood and is not afraid to be caught crying during a good read. When she's not reading or writing about bad boys, you can find her watching her favorite shows such as Sons Of Anarchy, Dexter and True Blood.

She is the author of Wake Up Call, This Regret, Slade, Hemy, Get Off On The Pain and Thrust and is currently working on more works for 2015.

Contact her on:

Facebook
Victoria Ashley Author and Victoria Ashley-Author

Goodreads
Victoria Ashley

Twitter
@VictoriaAauthor

Books by Victoria Ashley

Wake Up Call
This Regret

WALK OF SHAME
Slade (#1)
Hemy (#2)
Cale (#3) Coming 2015

PAIN
Get Off on the Pain
Something for the Pain (#2) Coming 2015

CPSIA information can be obtained
at www.ICGtesting.com
Printed in the USA
LVHW081016300121
677895LV00044B/1451